FALLING
FOR LOVE
AGAIN

Compiled and Edited by
Ravina Kaniyawala – Riya

FALLING
FOR LOVE
AGAIN

Compiled and Edited by
Ravina Kaniyawala – Riya

First
Step
Publishing
Paving Ways For New Writers

First Published in USA in 2016 by First Step Publishing
Editorial / Sales / Marketing Office at
303-304 Garnet Nirmal Lifestyles Ph 2
Behind Nirmal Lifestyles Mall
LBS Marg Mulund West
Mumbai 400080
E-Mail:- info@firststepcorp.com
www.firststepcorp.com

ISBN: - 978-93-83306-38-1
Publisher: Rohit Shetty
Compiled and Edited by: Ravina Kaniyawala – Riya
Branding, Marketing and Promotions by: Design Fishing
Digital Management by: First Step Corp
Typeset in Book Antique
Paperback: $ 10

Contents

Editor's Note

Hello, people ,This is me Ravina Kaniyawala Editor of the most awaited book 'Falling For Love Again'.

I feel lucky and honoured to be the editor of the anthology book which contains the 12 spectacular stories which are unique and different from each other. Each story will make you fall in love with the writing and telling ability. You will realise the feelings of love that you have felt for someone, somewhere and you lost them with time but story will tell you how that feelings get back to you and remind you of the special one.

You will get number of books on love in the market but this book is all about Falling In Love Once Again which gives you the actual reality that world face during love. The book will tell you how to fall for the person again, you will get many of love stories book but this book is all about hatred feelings, the situation where love fails but how they overcome and they fall in love again either with the same person or with the new person. The book will tell you the reality between the stories.

We, the team of Falling for Love again worked as a team for letting this anthology book turn into a real shape. We try to make this anthology book different and amazing to chase the success and we hope you will love it.

Have a great read
Fall in Love with the Book
Thank You

Kanak Aggarwal

Kanak Aggarwal , a 20-year-old Delhi-based guy, studying to be an engineer, has stepped into the world of writing in 2014 with his first book " A Letter From My Father" which was a bestseller and in 2016. He became a part of yet another bestselling anthology "If I Had A Last Wish" published by First Step Publishing .

Music is the first love of this budding writer. He is an intuitive guitarist, pianist, singer, and a composer as well.

Brought up in a very social environment, Kanak has amazing bonds with his family and friends.

He is an enthusiastic sportsman and a gym addict.

He is a pragmatic softie who aspires to say the unspoken social situations and unsaid feelings in relationships with his writing.

He usually attempts to sharpen the blurred lines between realism and emotions.

His writings reflect the ongoing irony in city life.

Arrange Some Love For Me

"You are an idiot. She is making a fool out of you. Stop spending some cash on her and the truth will unleash itself upon you." Said Manan in a very concerned tone.

"I don't know what's the problem between you guys," I said getting irritated because of his constant poking on my shoulder.

"She will definitely drop her pants for anybody if she gets a Gucci or Versace. She loves your cash, your warm, crunchy currency. Neither you nor your tool in your pants" Manan, my best friend, said while punching my shoulder.

"Firstly, that's my shoulder, not your punching bag. Secondly, no she won't. Thirdly, we are in a relationship from last 2 years Manan. I know her in ways that you can't even think of. " I said while preparing myself to give him an uppercut if he touched my shoulder one more time.

"Agreed. But firstly, you have been in a relationship only with her in the last two years. Did you hear me? Only is the keyword. Secondly, I have dated 9 girls in last 7 months itself. Thirdly, you will have to accept this fact that I am more experienced than you in every way because getting a girl in a relationship is not a child's game. It takes a lot of effort, blood, tears and sweat my friend. And when one's count of the girls he has dated reaches the point where he can't even remember it, you, he and everyone else is bound to accept and bow down in front of his glory. You know her very well, I know the whole community of girls very well. The girl you are dating is nothing but a greedy bitch" he kept his point firmly.

"Yeah whatever" I murmured.

"I will prove it to you. Just promise me that tomorrow you won't gift her anything. No matter what she asks for? I know you are a millionaire, but promise me, only for tomorrow. Please."

"Fine. Promise." I said and went away. He was getting intolerable and my intolerance was increasing equally. Couldn't risk him boycotting me like people were boycotting Aamir khan these days.

Manan was my childhood friend. With time I became stronger, a successful man, our bond grew up to be equally stronger and successful. We both knew the fact that no matter what happened to us, we always had each other's back. We followed the bro code, religiously. And since the first day that I got in a relationship with Mehek , Manan has been after my life, always telling me to break up with her. But I couldn't. I loved her, and honestly, I never could find even one reason about why Manan was so adamant about flushing her out of my life. Maybe he was scared that he might lose his importance. I don't know. She was beautiful. She made me happy. She made life look so beautiful and she was so god damn amazing in bed. How could I just leave her?

I was lost in these thoughts as I reached home. I knocked on the door and my mom opened it.

"Wow, Why did you come home so early? You should have stayed for a bit longer" she said. No actually, she taunted.

"Mom, it is only 10. That's really not even close to "being late" for someone who is 24."

"So what if you are 24? For me, you will always remain a kid. Now go and change. I will bring some dinner." She said and walked towards the kitchen.

"Mom, I love you." I murmured and went to freshen up.

When I came back she started the most dreaded topic for the guy who belongs to an orthodox family and is in a serious relationship with someone and who hasn't told about it to his parents because he is afraid that his mom might die with a heart attack and his dad might shoot him in the head. "Arrange marriage"

"If today you would have been married, you would have come home on time. You would have gone to office more regularly"

"Mom, please not again. Please, I beg you." I pleaded.

"She is right son. Get married now. We are old, and you are irresponsible." Said my dad in his forever blunt tone.

"I will let you know when I am ready. Please stop pestering me about this everyday" I said in a frustrated tone and walked back to my room.

How was getting married going to help me? I had everything, I had my parents, a lot of money, a super hot girlfriend, a best friend who would take a bullet for me. The only thing that I needed now was batman's suit.

Next morning after having my breakfast, I checked my cell phone. 39 missed calls. 1 from Mehek and 38 from Manan. I decided to call Mehek first. Yeah, yeah, I know what you are calling me right now, asshole right? Do I look like I care?

"Hey, baby, Up so early today?" I asked.

"I was missing you much . Good morning baby." She said in her usual sweet voice.

"Really? Let's go out somewhere then?"

"Let's go to the mall. I had selected a dress there yesterday. Thought I would show it to you before I buy it." She actually meant that before she shows me the dress and then I pay for it. This was the moment where I had to choose between the promise that I had made to my best friend and between the dress that my girlfriend wanted to buy. For the first time I decided not to be an asshole and I chose my best friend. So I made an excuse about mom's appointment at the hospital for her eye check-up which I had forgotten but now it suddenly remembered as I just made it up and fixed it after I decided not to break the promise I made. So the plan got cancelled and the call got dropped.

It was time to call Manan.

"38 missed calls. Are you alright? I was worried. The first thing I did after waking up was calling you." I lied, obviously.

"Listen am not Mehek. Am Manan. You can't fool me, man." He said it like it was very obvious that I was lying. Was it?

"Houston we have a situation. I need 30000 cash in my account right now. Don't ask any questions. Just do as I say. After 3 hours I will text you a location. Be there on time commando."

"I hope you are not in any kind of trouble. Are you?"

"No, it's just some ransom money. Am getting your life back". He said and disconnected.

What was that? I mean, call somebody, ask for 30000, shove some philosophy on his face, and disconnect. Man, my life was full of fucking crazy people. Super fucking crazy people. Every one of them.

I called my secretary and told her to transfer the money in Manan's account. And as he said, 3 hours later, he texted me a location. It was Mehek's apartment.

I quickly got into my car, and the streets of Delhi got one more wannabe street racer who imagined himself to be the Vin Diesel from The Fast and Furious when he was not even Uday Chopra from Dhoom. I drove to her apartment as fast as I could, at 60 km per hour. That's the fastest one can drive at 12 pm on Delhi roads.

I noticed I had another text from Manan telling me that the door was open and I should come straight in without knocking. I did as told to me. What I saw looked something like what I had seen in the porn flick last night. No, she was not riding him, she was sucking him …without her pants.

"I told you bhai , she would drop her pants for a Gucci. And guess what, you are the one who gifted it to her."

"But I didn't buy anything, I didn't even go out shopping with her because I had promised you…how could you do this to me Mehek?"

"Haha, I bought it, you only paid 30000 for it." He said while closing his fly." But you were right, she is amazing in bed. So still don't want to break up with her?"

I had no words. I was hurt. I never had a girlfriend in school or college, she was my first girlfriend and I found her giving a blowjob to my best friend. What the hell was

I supposed to say? What the hell was I supposed to do? I had already killed her thrice in my head.

"Let it be" I whispered and walked out.

I went back home and locked myself in my room.

I called Manan and bursted in tears in front of him. I told him I would always listen to him now. I told him I was sorry that I had been ignoring his warning from so long. I told him how much hurt I was.I told him I had no idea what to do now. He said just four words. "MOVE ON mere bhai"

Now I had to make a decision. I could sit there for days and cry over the girl who would have slept with someone else by now or I could have found someone better, someone, I deserved. I stood up, wiped my tears and walked straight into my dad's room.

" Dad, arrange some love for me," I said.

"I will arrange the person for you, but unfortunately, love my son, you will have to manage that yourself," he said and smiled.

My dad was a liar. He had already arranged the person. I mean, he had already decided weeks ago that to whom I was supposed to get married. The next day, we went to her house. No doubt the house was beautiful. We were three, and they were …just so many. They were treating me like I was some superstar. They made me eat so much, especially the sweets, so many of them. My stomach had started to ache. But my to be wife was nowhere to be seen. She was getting ready, most probably. Soon she walked out in a blue saree. She had long hair, a bit curly at the tips which reached up to her knees. Her lips glistened in the light of the lamps. I don't know if it was she who was walking slowly or it was the time that had slowed down. Her name was Riya. She was beautiful beyond words can describe. She was like the view of that rising sun which slowly lightens up your heart from the passage through your eyes. I looked at her agape.

Families chatted for a bit longer and then we came back home. I was thinking about her all the time. Mehek was hot, no doubt...but Riya, she was beautiful, elegant. She was the girl I would think twice before laying my hands on. I wouldn't want my dirty hands to reduce the worth of something so beautiful. My face clearly told my parents that I was ready to marry her. But for their satisfaction, they asked me, and I did say a yes. It was a yes from their side too and our wedding was arranged. I called Manan and told him "am getting married"

"Arrange marriage, seriously dude?"

"Why? What's wrong with it?" I asked.

"I don't know, I mean you will have to spend your life with someone you don't even know. You met her a day ago and next week it's your wedding. How much can you possibly get to know about her in a week?" He was worried.

He was right too. I liked her looks. I didn't know how was she as a person. But on the other hand, this idea excited me. I was about to live with a complete stranger under one roof. We were about to sleep on the same bed, share the same bathroom, have dinner together, go out for walks and try to talk to each other and get to know each other. Wait..right, "get to know each other". We would get to know each other, with time right? We will have a whole life to know each other now. Some of her things would surprise me, some of mine would surprise her. Two people who hardly knew each other , who belonged to completely different backgrounds, upbringing, completely different characters, were about to live in a lifelong committed relationship and sleep on the same bed, I had my whole life with me now to find reasons about why I should stay with this unknown someone. It looked like a challenge. Now when I thought of it, I liked the idea a little more than a little.

Our wedding was arranged. I looked at our wedding card "Sanjay weds Riya". I took a deep breath. She was about to leave her home forever now and would live with a total stranger. I looked at her. She was looking at the ground. Her face was covered in her pallu. I saw her hands, they were trembling. The loud music might have stopped her sobs from reaching my ears, but the teardrop that had fallen from her eye on her palm told me that she was scared too. She was confused as well. That's when I realised that it was me who agreed to get married like this and in a few minutes she would become my responsibility. I decided not to wait for those few minutes. I took her hand in mine. She was taken aback and looked at me with her wide eyes. I saw her eyes from so close for the first time. They were wet and were desperately holding back the ocean of emotions because they knew that if they went loose, the flood would drown everyone in them. I looked at her and smiled.

"I am scared too. I can't promise you anything about the future, But I can promise you one thing about myself

Riya, I don't know if we will fall in love or not, but I will be always there to protect you."

She stared at me like that for a few more seconds, like she was frozen. And then she decided to let go of all the emotions that her eyes were holding back. She clung to me and cried like a baby.

"You spoiled my sherwani" I joked. She smiled. I laughed. We got married.

After all the ceremonies got over, we went to my house. Oh, sorry, our house. Now this was a very complicated moment. For the first time I was confused about "should I initiate sex?" or" should I wait for her to give me a hint?" Should I carry a rose with me like they show in the movies? I had witnessed her in pain a few hours ago. Leaving her mom, dad, her family behind and settling down here with me, a complete stranger was a big thing and I was already respecting her courage and now she was about to sleep with the same stranger, naked. Trust me, her courage was actually turning me on. But the real question was what was all this? Was this a ritual, necessity, compulsion, being unfair or something else?

As I entered the room, I saw her sitting there. Her face covered with her pallu. I could see a faint shadow of her through that. I took a step forward and I noticed that she twitched the bed sheet with her toes. I took another step and she did it again. I smiled. Actually, I laughed. She cleared my confusion. Not about what all this was, but about what I had to do.

"Hey! Riya, listen, don't take me wrong, but I guess I will sleep on the couch tonight. And you sleep on the bed. "I said in my calmest tone ever.

"Did I do something wrong?" she said in a feeble, scared voice.

"No, you didn't, who said that. You are my wife Riya. I don't want us to sleep together when we don't even know each other. We will surely sleep together someday. Someday when both of us would want it. When we will know each other. I don't want to have sex with a stranger. I want to make love to my wife. "I smiled and said. I looked at her shadow, and I could figure out, that she was smiling too. I went to sleep on the couch when she called out to me from behind. I looked at her.

"You know what my mom told me? She said that I would fail as a wife if I would not sleep with you tonight. Thank you for proving her wrong. Good night. "She turned off the lamp. I knew that on the other side, her heart was in peace and her lips with a smile.

"Goodnight "I whispered.

From next day onwards, we started to open up with each other. I cooked breakfast for her and I could tell it from her face that she liked it. We both didn't share some very big secret of ours with each other but yes we started talking. Sometimes I saw the same expression on her face which I had seen that night when I slept on the couch and I would know that I had again proved her mom wrong on some point or maybe dad this time. But I never asked her, I had a hunch that someday she would tell me on her own. One day she finally did told me about the list of dos and don'ts that her mother had given her. I listened to them carefully and then I laughed crazily.

"Excuse my laughter Riya. But you have to remember these that you are in a new world now and in this world you are free to live the way you want to. You don't need a list of do's and don'ts here. So let go of your past and live in present with me. I will make sure that you live happily. "I smiled at her and touched her back to comfort her.

One night while watching a movie I casually asked Riya what she wanted to become. She hesitated a bit and after a few minutes, she whispered "singer, I wanted to become a singer"

I looked at her. The expression on her face was the evidence of this fact that how passionately she would have wanted to sing. Accidentally I had pulled some very painful strings of her heart.

Next morning at 10, the doorbell rang.

"Riya would you please open the door for me?" I shouted from inside the bathroom.

She opened the door to find a lady holding a harmonium. "Namastey, myself Mahalaxmi. I was called here to give singing lessons to Mrs. Riya." She said.

I peeped through the bathroom door and noticed a tear drop fall down from her eyes. I wrapped a towel around me and came out.

"Who was there Riya?" I called.

She came running towards me and hugged me tightly. We fell on the bed. She was kissing me incessantly.

"Don't you have a class to attend?" I said with a smirk on my face.

She kissed me again and went outside. Later that night I didn't have sex with a stranger. I made love to my wife and thanked my dad for getting me married to a stranger that day.

Somewhere between the tea and the evening snacks, somewhere between her college tales and her shopping lists , somewhere between the evening walks and the late night ice creams , somewhere between her unpredictable mood swings and my uncontrollable anger, somewhere between me getting sick and she taking care of me and she breaking her leg while trying to play basketball, somewhere between the long drives and the picnics, somewhere between the gossip that her eyes did with my lips and my lips did with her eyes....we fell in love.

I was sitting on the balcony of my farmhouse at goa. I saw Riya walking on the beach and enjoying the sun. "Is she walking slowly or is it the time that has slowed down? She is so beautiful. I can never have enough of her",I thought. Six months ago if life wouldn't have taken turns as it luckily did, maybe I would have never even met the love of my life.

Riya came back up and hugged me from back.

"Enjoying the day?" I asked.

"Yes, it's beautiful. Thank you for bringing me here. I am going to the kitchen. Am famished. You want anything?" she said.

"Yeah, arrange some love for me," I said. She smiled. I breathed.

Pooja Khurana

Pooja Khurana has done her Master's degree in English Literature and completed her B.Ed. degree. She is a teacher by profession and love being with kids. She is a contributing writer in three famous anthologies The Hidden Gems, Crush 2 and also a part of an International Anthology 'If I had a last wish, she has also scripted many stage plays for school. She loves to carve poetries and no. of poetries has been published in newspapers and magazines. She is an active member of Delhi's famous activity and poetry groups of Delhi.

She has gained many laurels from all quarters and following her heart has led her to fountains of happiness.

She believes that life is a miracle and being a true follower of her dad's teachings she dedicates her stories to her beloved dad.

The Touch

'Yes! Stella, You can trust me, Please tell me why can't you marry me?'

"Don't you think I am worthy of your love?" questioned Sameer

"No, No Sameer... it's not about you, it's about me and what happened to me."

"I am so glad that I have a friend like you, someone who loves me, but trust me I won't be able to reciprocate your love, I am not an answer for your pious love"... and Stella started to cry.

"Stella I need to know"

Stella sobbed and slipped down the memory lane where it all happened...

The dark room was scared to hear the panting sound, the sweat was swirling behind the ear and continuous sobbing hindered the deadly silence of the night. Tears were rolling down the cheek and heart was trying to catch enough oxygen to keep up the breath, suddenly someone opens the door

"Stella...Stella, What are you doing here...?"

Stella ran and hugged her mother, but couldn't say a word, she was all wet with her sweat, her mother couldn't make out what went wrong and Stella too had no idea what she went through.

It all started when one day she was playing in her room and her father's friend saw her and entered her room.

"Hey, Stella have some chocolates."
"You are a cute little kid"… dark man said rolling his lusty eyes.

His hands were moving on her body, but that ten-year-old kid was quite unaware of his intentions, but she definitely knew that the touch is not the friendly one.

"Come on baby play with uncle."

And his despicable body overshadowed the little kid, she tried to escape but that bulky body was strengthy enough to fulfil his heinous intentions .Now whenever he used to come to her house, she used to feel the chills in her body. One day she tried to explain everything to her mom, but her mom denied saying,

"Uncle Loves you, baby, he comes here to play with you"

So it continued for months, that broke her apart and left her emotions naked , sadly there was nobody to listen to her, nobody responded except that cruel disgusting demon with a cruel smile on his face.

School teacher was also complaining about her grades, her health was also showing up, Stella's parents were really worried about her, but had no clue about the real reason, and Stella too was unable to share the deep-seeded reason, as she knew nobody will believe her, she knew it was wrong and should not tolerate it, but she had no choice. Slowly these incidents took over her daily life, she was so emotionally shattered that wherever she used to go she felt the insecurity rushing down her spine, she felt that everybody is talking about her, how bad she is.

Days were passing by and the abuse continued. She didn't want to go to school but her mother forced her.

One day teacher asked her to get some chalks, Stella stood up and moved towards the table, but suddenly she fainted, everybody was surprised what must have happened to her.

"Stella Stella…what happened?" Teacher shouted.

"I don't know I was feeling very weak, and I fell down" Stella replied

"When you don't feel fine, why can't you just say no?" The teacher gave her a pensive look.

"LEARN TO SAY NO"

The teacher said so many things to her but what her mind heard that time was, "Learn to say no".

Same night when she witnessed the shadow again , as he unbuttoned his intentions Stella shouted "no". she shouted her lungs out and repeatedly shouted "NO" "NO" "NO"…

Her parents banged, opened the door and were horrified to see the whole thing.

Stella was crying and badly shivering, the man ran away.

"I am so sorry my child, we couldn't save you, we couldn't protect you" Stella's mother sobbed.

Stella was relieved and happy that finally she overcame those demonic consequences.

It's been said that wounds do heal up but scars do remain, so Stella was still in a shock even today, and Sameer could sense that easily as Stella was still shivering while sharing that unfortunate experience and Sameer wanted her to be out of the clutches of that emotional captivation at any cost.

I know it's been hard for you Stella, but enough. I just want you to be free from that.

Do you trust me? Sameer asked!

Yes... said, Stella!

Come with me, do as I say!

Sameer then asked her to write whatever comes into her mind on each chit, he had 5 chits and Stella wrote HATE, DARK ROOM, TOUCH, TEARS, and FEAR. Sameer tied all those cards to those balloons and asked her to let those go away in the sky. Stella was silently watching them disappear in the sky and tears were rolling down her cheeks.

"These were your worries, Stella, they will never come back" Sameer smiled. Sameer took her hand and assured her that she will be ok, and Stella could easily feel the friendly healing touch and slowly she felt she was forgetting the touch that earlier jolted her inside out. They both smiled and walked towards the sea and Sameer was hopeful that Stella is now walking towards a new dawn.

I never thought I could love again, I never thought I could let any touch my body. My body could not stand any emotion as I became too weak, really weak after that unfortunate incidence happened to me. But I always knew that someone will understand me someday. And I am one of those fortunate ones who found herself dipped in the ripples of love with someone who is as worthy as one's man should be. I can now acclaim that miracles do happen as I saw my life story started happily.

Sanjana Bandooni

Sanjana Bandooni (Born 27th September 1996). She is a prolific blogger and loves to blog on a different topic related to the society. She is an amateur writer who loves imagining and writing stories since her childhood and won many prizes at school and college level.

Presently she is pursuing Bachelor of Commerce from M.K.P P.G College, Dehradun.

She loves reading romantic and thriller stories. She is a diehard fan of John Green, Nicholas sparks, and Durjoy Datta.

She has ventured into published writing recently and trying to do decent work in the literary world.

She can be contacted at www.sanjanabandooniii.blogspot.com
Mail Id – bandooniii@gmail.com.

Brimmed Love

It was not until too late when she realized that there is nothing more beautiful than an ordinary love. A love that holds your hand and walks with you when the world is in greys. A love that recognises the flaws in your eyes, all your perfections and imperfections and makes to attempt to alter the shine in your eyes.

A love that carries your sadness like it belongs to the surroundings. A love that talks more about the actions and less with showering words. A love that won't let darkness shadow you and let glitter dazzle. A love that carries your heart always and protect it with devotion.

Once in a lifetime, we cross paths with someone who make us realise what it feels like having someone to share those feelings, that undefined bond. All letters, words, phrases fall short of meanings when it comes to express those emotions.

Diya and Tanmay both were like the opposite poles but charming and beautiful. Tanmay was too much talkative and a nerdy guy while Diya was silent, calm and serene as night.

They were neighbours and were in the same college too , pursuing the same course B.TECH (CSE) from Delhi College of Engineering.

Tanmay Singh, a guy famous for his pranks in the whole college with so many friends around him. A guy with the perfect physique and graceful dynamism captures everyone's heart easily.

One fine day, after attending all the classes, before lunch break Diya was moving to the cafeteria.
On her way, he stopped her.
He quizzed, "Diya, why you're so calm always? You don't even reply to my pranks in the class."
Diya replied in a low voice, "There is nothing such that. I just don't want to be in any verbal fight with you."
He was taken aback. Perhaps he was smitten by the way words rolled off from her lips. Their eyes met and he got an indication. A change which he had been waiting forever.
He looked in her eyes with a question on his lips.

Diya started looking here and there as she didn't want to open the secrets of her life with anyone.
Tanmay asked something different this time. "Have you ever been in love or you're a hopeless romantic girl?"
Diya replied in an agitated way.
"I heard what you said. I'm not the silly romantic you think or the type of girls who roam around you. I don't want the heaven or the shooting stars. I don't want any precious gemstones or beautiful expensive gifts. I have those things already. I want a steady hand.
A kind soul. I want to fall asleep and wake up knowing my heart is safe. I want to love and to be loved."
He was numb at that time. Those words from Diya left a deep imprint on his heart and soul. Somewhere inside

the mischievous guy, there is a pure and innocent soul where the chord struck this time.

Love blossoms in the spring like the rosebud. Pranks were changed to casting a sidelong glance at her, adoring her most of the times.

Tanmay started doing silly things in front of her to make her laugh, to make her comfortable in his presence.

He started to write about those feelings which people read in novels. The silent adoration changed to the blissful feelings of love.

Sometimes in between the lectures, a cacophony of voices, laughter and smile. Her one look, their eyes met which sends him into the world of nocturnal lights.

Tanmay took her as she's without any prejudice. It was going to be something magical this time, the love started to bloom from both sides.

She penned it in her diary one day about 'Falling in love again.'

I am never being good enough. I am always torn with scratches. I always carry a tiny spec of sadness in my heart. I have many untold stories to write and to traced by someone, but they are insignificant to you. If you ask about my feelings and giving a chance to love again, expect an honest answer from me. I will either love you too much or will be too dramatic with you.

I have many flaws, I do mistakes and I have sharp edges too, but I know how to love and how to stay with love."

After a span of two weeks, they planned a meeting on the terrace at night.

That Night -

The clock showed 2:00 A.M. They were sitting on the terrace under the baby blue sky.

"Look at us. Who would have thought that we would be sitting together someday like this?" , she said while looking at the sky. "Did I tell you I love full-moon nights? It is magical out here!"

"What if I didn't show my feelings, you know, people have told me that I do that too often, and without uttering a single word", he held her hand in his hands and looked at her from the corner of his eyes. She was still busy in admiring the moon.

"Sometimes you're like an innocent kid who makes mistakes. For all we know, I might do it. What we're having here is not real?"

"Stop over thinking just be here with me. Look into my eyes. Now look at the moon, will you?"

He looked at the crescent moon, "I am glad that you're here with me", he whispered.

"I will be with you. Always."

The crescent moon night was never too gorgeous than this in the near past.

When she pulled back herself from the magical encounters, where Tanmay and her breaths touched each others. Tanmay stayed calm. He smiled in a brilliant way and tucked her straight hair strand behind her left ear. Her phone beeped, a message with warm feelings popped up on the screen.

He summarised his feelings and love in few words putting there perfectly.

"The definition of love is elusive for me. No one can define it. But in the end I know one thing for sure, for me, love is you and everything related to you. I am in love and carried it as a magic; the glittering image of your eyelashes, irresistible and magical. "

"I want to turn the knots of your soul and peep through the windows of your eyes. Please let me? I've been to countless places, and none of them have ever felt like home to me like your cosy arms. Please let me embrace you? I will heal every little broken place as many times as I possibly could until my heart skipped."

His words made a great impact on her. As she too never thought that someone (off course other than Chirag) would be able to win her heart as easily.

She really wished that Chirag would have told her something like this ever. She is a bit tired now from these thoughts, especially since the day he announced that he had found someone for him.

Diya was a little bit busy in doing her assignments; after putting her phone on the side table, she suddenly started thinking about Chirag.

'I should clarify my feelings to Chirag for once. I don't think that I will be able to love or even like someone else until I am not clear about what I want', she penned out her thoughts in her diary.

'But why should I clarify? What is there to clarify something? Chirag had already conveyed that he is in a relationship. And, as far as I know him, he will love her until the end. What am I dreaming of and expecting? And if I am not able to get over Chirag, why did I walk into Tanmay's life? What am I doing?'

She felt weak and tears trickled down from her eyes. What a destiny it is? She told to herself, that someone has just accepted his feelings for her, but she's not able to reciprocate as she's in dilemma to withdraw herself from someone else, who has already found somebody for him. She wiped off her tears as soon as she saw her mother.

"What happened to your eyes? Have you cried? Everything okay na *beta*?"
"Yes, mamma. Everything's fine", Diya replied.
She was on her bed, when she checked her phone again, there was a message from Tanmay.

"I don't know how to write the magic I experienced today. I think of us holding hands, arms around each other, the strolls through the city, getting ice-cream and chocolates- all those hours in between hectic days when we could be happy to just look into each other's eyes. Imagine your voice and prettiest smile when you would get excited by my little surprises, describing the smallest things and your dark black eyelashes, the way they would open and close. I will make sure and do it forever for you, to make you cheerful, because I love you."

Life was no more a dilemma; after a week and she was constantly in touch with Tanmay.

*****Two months later*****

'How can I think like that?'

After looking at the full moon from her balcony and after feeling those special moments again with Tanmay, she had to scold her heart silently. This was the first time. She was still holding the love which has already left. That guilt of cheating Tanmay is sweeping her fully now a day but Tanmay has found her princess in Diya. She can't control her feelings and emotions, especially when they meet.

She is in a constant dilemma of choosing her love. On one side, there a guy who already left her and on the another side, there is Tanmay; who was trying his best to win her heart and to let her smile again. Sometimes she gets angry with herself and sometimes she feels guilty. The more she wants to come out of this web of emotions, the more she is sucked into it.

"Diya beta, please come inside. It's too late", her father said and she switched off the lights of the balcony and came into her room.

Diya Ahuja, at the age of 20 with a medium height and a chubby cute face; was blessed with dimples, long wavy hairs, thick wide eyes. No one can easily take off his eyes from her. Being the only child of her parents, she enjoys every luxury of life and still her heart is nowhere.

This story is all about Diya, Chirag and Tanmay. Diya and Chirag, both were neighbours from the age of five. He is a year older than her. At the age of five and even now at the age of twenty, she's not sure that how come Chirag was so mature and calm. Not to mention that they became friends easily and started sharing not only toys but the dinners too. Being in the same school gave them an opportunity to spend more time with each other while travelling to school. In their school bus, they used to discuss anything and everything with their presence and curiosity. Chirag used to protect her from everyone and face all the problems of her life.

Time flew and years passed; childhood turned into teenage but they were the same. She still loved to play basketball in the courtyard and he still used to pull her hair when she could not solve his maths equation.

Despite her mother's dislike about spending with Chirag. She used to spend her evenings only with him. They both used to ride bikes to visit the nearby pond. They park their bikes and would sit on the bench and walk like lovers. They both used to talk everything under the silent sky. She never felt any kind of hesitation while talking to him and Chirag too never treated her like a simple girl. For him, she was his best friend and for her, he was her hero.

She was seeing herself falling for him more and more with each passing day. On the other hand, he was still in the stage of friendship where he would openly share his feelings for that beautiful girl who is his best friend.

As dawn pours on her doorstep, her dreams were shattered too. She still remembers that evening. The evening which came with an unexpected news which changed their lives completely.

When unexpected things happened, how anxious she felt. And, how she tried to overcome that 'UNEXPECTED'?

The evening when she was engrossed in reading a novel 'Nothing last forever' by Sidney Sheldon while lying on her bed.

She heard a knock on her door. This was something unusual for her as there was no need for her parents to knock her bedroom door. And Chirag, he had never done this. He used to shout her name and then he used to enter the room. With preoccupied thoughts about the story in her mind, she got up and opened the door.

He came in silently and stood there; still without saying any single word. It was annoying for her, that firstly he disturbed her while when she was reading the book of her favourite author. She had to put her book on the side table and turned to him. He was still looking at her. She raised her eyebrows and silently asked with her eyes, "What?", to this, he came forward and hugged her tightly. It was something she didn't expect. She was not sure whether to cherish this moment when her dream guy was around her arms or should felt the critically regarding the news he was about to say.

Whatever it was, the tight hug was still stuck tightly on her body and that feeling. No words in the world can explain that feeling.

She closed her eyes and wrapped her hands around his shoulders. She was still wondering about what was happening and why, but the moment was so precious that she allowed her heart to completely beat and match with his heart beats rhythmically and asked her mind to stop thinking odd things.

He somehow managed to express his feeling and the unexpected news he was about to say. After few moment, he slowly unwrapped his hands around her and with an almost shaky voice he confessed, which led to destroy her dreams completely.

"Diya, our family is moving to Mumbai as my father has got his urgent transfer letter," Chirag said.

It felt like thousands of nails had entered in her body after what he said. She felt like she was completely broken as she saw darkness ahead her without him. He held her hands but by that time, tears rolled down her cheeks. When he tried to console her, she burst into tears. He too accompanied her. Yes, he was also crying.

Crying at the thought of getting separated. She never in her dreams thought of this scene in her life. He told her that his father informed him in the morning. They were moving in a week and the span is very less.

Before she could respond or speak, she heard her mother shouting at her. Surely she had started thinking something wrong. Chirag left her hands and ran towards the door.

"Diya, meet me tomorrow at the bus stop same time."

That evening she was not able to eat anything. It felt like something was blocked in her heart and choked her heart and throat so she was feeling numb. The thought of being away from Chirag, when her heart was already started loving was completely heart wrenching.

She saw her mother happy as she must have got the news about Chirag and his family is moving to Mumbai. Her father, although kept asking her about why she was sad. He tried to explain and console her that friends come and go as life is long. Who would tell him that Chirag was more than a friend for her?

Next day, after seeing her puffy, red eyes at the bus stop where they reached fifteen minutes earlier every day. Chirag tried again to console her. His idea was about to be in touch via Skype, phone calls, facebook and emails. This sounds joke to her. She could not able to speak anything , else her eyes responded with tears. She wasn't sure whether he had the same pain in his heart. She wasn't sure how she was going to overcome this sadness and separation. With the moist eyes, they departed each other with lots of memories and love.

- Present

After a gap of six months, they met on the terrace again.

"I don't want to talk to you this way, you know?"

They were sitting on the terrace. Through the clouds, moonlight shimmered on the left side of her face. A cold yet slow breeze gently caressed her hair and the silence between them filled with half-baked love and self-realization.

"What do you mean?" He asked without realising that his voice, by now, had become loud. He was seeing her after six months. Memories flooded his mind and a terrible sense of longing gripped him. They avoided eye contact and kept staring the moon.

Diya was out of the town from the last six months. And she was not even replying the text and calls from Tanmay. She wants to keep herself in solitude for some time. As she was in constant dilemma to fall in love again or choose to stay with the memories of Chirag.

"I was missing you even though you were sitting right beside me. The realisation that you don't love me was pulling my guts out, and that is not how I wanted to remember you."

"So, that's why you just left?" He blurted with an anguish that shook her entire body. She looked at him and didn't speak a word. The night was on the verge of getting lost now drenched in the silence of an unrequited love."

If you know me even a bit, you will know that I never really left. I was just keeping myself away from you so that you can live without me and my love. Tell me something, do you still care about me?" She asked while looking into my eyes nervously.

"I never stopped caring," he said plainly and hugged her.

They were looking into each other eyes, and lips met. She was barely lifting her feet. Blush carved her face. It felt as if something is magical inside her is glittering in her eyes. All the while, I was trying to look into her eyes -- but she kept closed them. "

What are you so scared of?" He asked and let out a deep sigh. She lifted those long eyelashes to look at him and then she parted her lips from his. She intently stared into his eyes as if searching for something. "I feel that one day you're going to leave me."

He stayed quiet. The right words deceived Sometimes, people say things we never thought they will say. She slowly took his hands into hers. With their fingers intertwined, they made a silent resolve fight through things coming between them.

He looked at her. She had a half-smile on her face with moon glow. Hell, even on the best days, He doesn't understand her completely. However, even on the worst ones, He doesn't stop loving her intensely.

All we want is someone who will take a step ahead with us.

Diya was right in terms of accepting Tanmay's as a person who will correct her mistakes and still walk with her. Someone with whom the conversations is as effortless as breathing. Someone with whom she doesn't have to think twice before pouring out her being. Someone who might fail to love her on some days, but who will never stop trying. Someone who will never give up no matter how dark the night.

All she want is someone who can make her believe that, even though it is hard, but in a way -- it is still possible.

And Tanmay is that someone for her. "

Diya I'm not perfect and so my love It's not even close to perfection. It is messy, clumsy and too often it doesn't know where it wants to go.

My love locks itself in the room of longings and doesn't open the door for days.

Sometimes my love doesn't know when to stop. Sometimes I get scared and petrified. My love doesn't know when to stop giving. "

 I love you with all your flaws. I love you perfectly and imperfectly. You're the answer to all my prayers. With you, I felt safe, secure and contented. And I will never ask for more and love intensely. He brushes back the light brown hair studying her face. Deep dimples appear as she smiles back her eyes with mascara bright and beautiful.

At that moment he couldn't say anything to her. He just felt her hands on his hair, and in that brisk moment of intimacy, their sadness was melting away. She looked at him and let out a sigh.

Despite everything, they fall in love again moment by moment.

He leans forward to kiss her forehead. The darkness of night gets glowed with the warmth of his lips on her forehead.

Diya was hard to love but Tanmay had realised that already. She knows it very well that he choose to admire her gorgeous and terrifying parts too. A person without flaws won't be the same person as before.

Moonlight played with her in gorgeous ways. He had no idea what he did to deserve someone with so much grace. Maybe this is what they call 'Love'..

Manoj Kr Tigga

A civil engineer by profession and a shy guy by nature. Manoj was introduced to writing a few years back during his early twenties when he started writing poems. Few of his poems were published in local newspaper.

Manoj currently is trying to learn the art of story writing and explore more in the world of stories. He wants to express his feeling and thoughts through short stories and desires to write some novels in the coming years.

His story "The Last Chapter" is published in an anthology titled "The master Stroke" by Write India publisher. Also another story "Divine Dhaak Beat" has been in among the top 50 entry in the Bengal write ahead contest organised by Kolkata bloggers which will soon come in the form of a book.

Manoj is a music lover as well and whenever he gets some free time he is busy with his guitar and Hindi songs.

He also writes lyrics for his songs and tunes composed with his guitar.

"Falling in Love once Again"

She was back. It was the same place which she had left 3 months before with a firm decision of never returning back to him.

She looked at the surrounding. Everything looked silent. The house seems to be like a stranger. The wall of the room appeared like questioning her – who are you? The colours of the wall were same as earlier but looked faded. The large painting portraying a woman was hanged there on the eastern wall of the drawing room was as it is. Everything in the house was like more or less the same when she left. Only it looked a little unorganised with some stuff lying at an undesirable place. She felt like entering a new place. She looked at each corner of the house. Everything was familiar to her yet she felt something unfamiliar. She came outside the room in the balcony attached to her bedroom.

The pink rose plant in the vessel whose leaves used to be so green looked a little pale now. She looked at the sky. The horizon was reddish. It was the time to sunset.

She entered her bedroom. The bed which was perpendicular to the north-south direction in the south corner of the room was now shifted to the east corner. She looked at the photo frame which was kept at the side table of the bed. It was blank without a photo. She took it in her hand. Dust was there on the glass of the photo frame. The sky blue colour with a fish embedded in the frame was broken. She sat on the bed. Kept the photo frame in her lap and looked quietly. She can see a blur reflection of her face in the glass.

It was dusty. She tried to clean it with her hand. She remembers that it contained a beautiful smiling picture of her with him in a romantic pose standing closer to her. it was one of the pictures of their honeymoon. The broken frame without picture brought tears to her eye. She felt more lonely. Everything was fresh in her memory. The flashback started moving in her eyes.

The day when she left. It was still fresh in her memory. They had a hot argument with each other. In the course of it, they literally fought and he threw the photo frame on the floor, which broke. She kept frame back at the table. She remembers her last few days in the house with him before her departure.

It became hard and difficult for her to accept that her Love cum arranged marriage was so unsuccessful. She has always thought and believed that love is always unconditional without any if and buts. Unfortunately, her marriage life does not bring her the wishes and dreams which she expected. She failed and an unsuccessful marriage life made her believe that romantic marriage life is an illusion. The best days of their love and marriage life was no more when he used to do little sweet things which make her feel special. The frequency of surprise gifts and other romantic pretty activities soon became less and finally disappeared from their life. She cannot believe that there was a time when she used to tell her friends and relatives about the care and love which he offered for her. There was hardly any good thing left in her life to talk about.

She tried to understand – what went wrong? Her deteriorating relationship with him had left her shattered. Love has vanished from their life. They used to have frequent arguments over small likes and dislikes. It was only one year of their marriage and they realised that they are not meant for each other. Daily fight & frequent drama finally led her to decide to go to her home, leaving everything behind.

She remembers the day and date when she left. It was the last day of February. But now it's summer time. Everything is dry and so the relationship between them.

She sat quietly in the bed. Her eyes were dull with many thoughts that were coming and leaving to her mind. Was it her correct decision to come back? she asked herself.

She did not want to come back but her parents forced her to get back and give life one chance to make everything in place. Today her father dropped her in the house and left.

****

The doorbell broke the series of thoughts in her mind. It was the time for him to come back from office. She opened the door. It was him standing at the door. She looked at his face. It was a surprise for him. His eyebrows shrieked a little with his mouth a little open. He wanted to speak something but his words got disappeared in the mouth. She also did not say anything. She just gave him the way to enter the house.

He kept the keys of the car in the wall hanger. Placed his mobile on the dining table and entered the washroom. She closed the door and Her eyes followed him quietly.

49

She went to the kitchen and looked for the glass of water. He too entered the kitchen. But before she can, he took the water in a glass and he opened the door of the refrigerator, he took a bottle and gulped the water hurriedly and went for changing his clothes.

She kept standing in the kitchen. After some thought, she made coffee for him and put it near the chair where he was sitting in the bedroom without saying anything. They both remained silent and did not even tried to talk with each other. After some time, she entered the kitchen for preparation of dinner.

It was time to sleep. He was lying at one end of the bed facing opposite to her. She was also there at the other end of the bed. She turned her face and looked at him. He is still facing the wall on the other side. She also turned to other side and closed her eyes. The night came and went without a word between them. She opened her eye in the morning with the sound of an alarm coming from his mobile.

He made it silent and got up. She also got up and said – good morning. He gave a look at her for a few second but did not reply. After becoming free from nature call and getting fresh. She was busy in the kitchen for preparing breakfast. He got himself busy with newspaper. They silently took their breakfast and he left for office.

Days came and went between them just like that for a week, without talking. Both maintained distance and silence between them. The only time they came close was during the evening when the doorbell rang when he returned from office and she opens the door.

The distance between them can be felt by the silence of the house. They did not spoke a word to each other. The only thing they were doing was the daily routine. She cooked food, cleaned the house and clothes. He brings the stuff required for the kitchen and other daily needs. The only thing which looked arranged in the past few days was the house. The things were looking arranged at their desired location. The house was looking like home now.

Days were passing slowly. It was Sunday. In the morning, alarm clock did not ring. When she opened her eyes it was 8 am. She looked for him in the house but he was not there. When she came to open the door to look outside, she noticed at paper placed at the door which read – "Market".

He brought fish and some sweets from the market. He knows, she like fishes the most. When she was in the kitchen he came to her and gave a piece of paper to her which read - "I will make today". He prepared the breakfast and lunch that day. They still said nothing to each other. She felt that he wanted to say something. But he did not, neither she. The whole day they spent together in the house doing their own stuff without talking a word.

In the night before sleeping, she kept a paper near his pillow with a note written -"Fish was good" with a smiley. Written Communicating with having each other in front was something new which they liking and which was making way for them to open up.

He came to bed, read the message and a smile crossed his face. He lay in the bed. They were lying in the bed facing the ceiling. The distance between them in the bed was less compared to other days. The Moment of silence between them seems to be tired and looked faded. Both wanted to break the silence but they let it continued. Finally, after few moments when he turned toward her, his feet touched with her feet. He showed that he did not care, but his body became still. He wanted to move his legs away but cannot. The power of physical touch after such a long time induced a feeling of completeness to both. They desired for more. She moved her hand toward him and touched his hand and took his hand in her.

He was still silent. After a moment he turned his face toward her and pressed her hand. For the first time in last few days, they have touched each other. It was becoming difficult for both of them to suppress the hormones releasing by biological desire. Finally, they came close to each other and looked at each other face. Their eye met and got froze. They were looking at each other.

He wrapped her under his arm. She also hugged her as they came closer. Their heart beat raised. They felt that they were touching each other for the first time. Their lips touched each other and they forgot everything. They hugged and felt each other like never before. The warmth of physical wave which generated in their body reached its peak slowly and finally got silent like a melted ice. They lay side by side holding their hand.

He asked for the first time. "Why you went away"?

She replied – you made me do all these. Why you don't stop me from going away?.

He put his finger on her lips making her silent and said: "Don't say anything let the silence do its magic".

The silence made them silently accept each other in each other's arms. They both decided to allow the silence to do more magic in their life. Both became quite and slept quietly in each other's arm.

****

Next morning came with a beautiful smile on their face. She prepared his favourite puri raazma for him and they took their breakfast together. Before leaving the office he hugged her.

Alone in the home, She was arranging his wardrobe when she got a piece of paper cutting off some magazine. It was an article written about marriage and relationship. She started reading it.

Marriage is also like exploring the strength, the weakness, the interest and the passion between the couple to carry forward in their life. Off course priorities and responsibilities come between the emotional desire. But sometimes one has to overlook to keep going. Any relationship doesn't last because it was destined to, it last because two people decide and choose to continue irrespective of imperfection.

In this world nobody and nothing are perfect. It is impossible to find a couple who do not fight, it is also impossible to find a flawless couple.

Love and emotion are integral part and essence of any relationship. Everyone invests so much in emotion in any relationship so it's obvious to get hurt when expectation doesn't fulfil.

Love is always blind it can't see anything. But in marriage, one has to behave like a blind sometimes. You see the mistakes but you have to ignore it and accept the person. You just can't go away. It is essential to make your marriage life moving on. The true test of marriage lies in nurturing the desire to live with the same person and develop your love for each other despite the limitations. Marriage is all about two different people trying to find common ground.

The article left her emotionally drenched. She felt mentally stronger. Her decision of coming back for her marriage appeared correct and logical to her. She waited for the evening when he will come back.

****

In the evening he came. He brought a pair of pink rose of her favourite colour and kept in the glass half filled with water.

She did not say anything to him, but he noticed a smile on her face. Sometimes actions are stronger than words. Messages are conveyed and transmitted without a word. She just went near the flower, touched them gently and adjusted the position of the flower.

They are living together with less talking, sometime talking with sign language and communicating with moving their heads up & down and sometimes swinging it sideways. With each passing days, they were coming closer. The past grievances were slowly vanishing from their life. They were enjoying the new way of living together with less talking.

It was fourth Sunday for them together. After lunch, he came to her and asked her – if she wants to go for a new movie which is doing well.

She gave her approval with a smile. They were out of the house together after a long time. After the show, on their way back to the home he stopped the car in front of a restaurant and looked at her. She wanted to have dinner outside but could not tell him. When he asked her she just smiled and touched his hand.

They entered the restaurant and sat on the Lawn in the open area. At the corner, there was an old couple. They were sitting calmly talking to each other. They looked so relaxed and their age indicates that they have completed all their responsibility of life.

She looked at them and told him. I had always imagined and wished my life to be like them with you. But now I really don't know that this type of moment will ever come in my life?

He replied – "I also want to grow older with you. I wanted to see you on my side when I open my eye every morning. I want you to be there walking with me covering my entire journey of life."

She replied – "who don't want these little things in life. I think all married couple wish to have a life like what you said. I also wished and wanted you to support me in every dull and brighter moment of my life. I wanted to rest my head on your shoulder with my eye closed, whenever I felt to do so. I also wanted to be there for you and support you in every possible way. "

He – "you know, actually you gave me some of the best moment of my life. Which I will never forget."

She – "First three months of our marriage were really good. I doubted myself sometimes that I am really that much lucky to have got such a life partner. You really cared for me and I felt your love."

He-"I always tried to be for you and your only. But you know there are so many other things. Two people are always happy with each other. But when priorities and responsibilities came in between, one cannot give 100 % to only one person."

She – "I like it very much when you say like this. But it tough to apply when it comes to practical."

He –" how life goes, You have to see good and bad thing from the equal point of view. But it's human nature to get biased when it comes to giving priority to other things over their own interest and emotion."

She –" I don't want to say more. Tell me one thing where is our relationship going? Are we going to continue it? Are you ready to give yourself other chance with me in your life?"

He – "we will start everything from the beginning. We will give one fresh chance to understand each other. "

She – "beginning is already over and you know it was not that good. "

He – "you know when you left. I was in such a stage of my life when I can't imagine myself without you. When you left, something inside me wanted to live with you again. I missed you badly. It was so relief for me to see you back at home."

She – "you missed me, then why not you called me or even came to me to bring me back."

He – "I wanted to go to you many times but I was not sure that you will come. I am really thankful to you for coming back."

She -"I think what happened was good for us. At least we realised each other's importance in our life. Life has its own way of teaching us. "

They were interrupted with their order being placed at the table. They had their dinner. On the way back to the home, they don't spoke much.

****

Next day morning when he got up she was not there in the bed.

He looked for her. There she was standing on the balcony looking at the rising sun in the sky. He came close to her and hugged her. She kept her head on his chest.

She took his hand in her hand and said – "I want to live happily with you. I don't want to be away from you. I wanted to break my marriage with you, but I came back here for my parents. They asked me to give one chance to my life. I came here for one month only. Today it's over now and I don't even realise it. "

He took her face in his hand and kissed her on the forehead and said –"I will not let you go anywhere now."

He then took her under his arm. It was the best morning for them.

Then he took her inside the room. She said she will stay with him forever now. She asked him to put their old picture in the photo frame which was broken during their fight.

Everything was making way for its place. Love was slowly finding its way back in their life. Happiness rolled back to their home.

She started getting calls from him during his office time. She began to wait for his arrival from office. During his way back from office, the flower shop became his frequent stoppage. Weekends and holidays were once again being planned for outing and shopping.

Days passed, a week passed, months passed. Summer was at its departure making way for the monsoon to shower its love and freshness and give birth to life. It was one cloudy evening. A cool breeze was moving slowly. They both were sitting on the balcony with coffee mugs in their hand. Looking at each other they both were busy planning for their life.

Sheena Bassi

Sheena Bassi is an enthusiastic person with a never say die attitude. She has been an observer and an avid reader since childhood. After completing her M.B.A, she took her first step for being an author with her debut novel "Desire… holds the secret to change your destiny". She is also a contributing author of "Arranged to love". She is an active founder member of an N.G.O. Apart from this, she is also an entrepreneur. She currently resides in U.P.

Lost Girl ... Who could be found in books.

He pushed me towards the wall, his breath was heavy and his touch was enough to transform me to another world. We both were ravenous for each other so, the struggle to control our emotions proved useless. I wanted to shout but his lips locked mine and he was strong enough that I gave up. The truth was even I wanted him as I discovered I was the one he ever loved.

"You were the one I loved and I waited for you from the day you disappeared.

I love you my lost girl," he said trying to catch his breath.

****

Having to leave home is one of the worst things that can ever happen to someone. For me the idea of shifting to another city; completely unknown to me wasn't cool and that also for some stupid classes. But the lack of options made me go for it. So, there I was all alone staring people who were moving back and forth on the Chandigarh station. I started moving towards the exit, hitting those who were coming into my way through my bags hanging over my shoulder I took a pre-paid taxi. It took me half an hour to reach the given address. After paying him, I went in. The owner showed me my room which was for only one person, as no extra space, no fuss about keeping it clean, and no irritating stuff. After six hours of the torturous train journey, all I wanted was a shower and a sleep.

Next day was all new, I made to the coaching centre on time. I sat down beside a girl who was busy writing something. I looked at her with an intention to say hey but she was so engrossed in doing something so, I quit the idea. After a while, a lady entered which happened to be our C++ teacher. It was the first class and I was glad I hadn't missed anything.

I started dwelling in my routine, teachers were good but students were only concerned about their studies and had an unfriendly attitude. I thought to tolerate this and confined to only hey- hello's as I was there for a few months only. The place where I was a tenant was even more boring as most of the others were working as well. I was all alone, busy with my classes and studies. Classes had only started so there wasn't so much to study so that I could get myself indulge in my course books all the time. I thought of doing a part time job but again the schedule for classes kept on changing so it was hard to do that. Finally, I decided to escape from my boring life in books. I loved reading since I was a child.

So, I decided to devote almost my entire Sunday to the nearby bookstore as it did have a beautiful set up for readers, one could sit and read free of charge without interruption. Mr Danish who was of almost fifty years was a gentleman and courteous; another guy who worked part time was almost three or four years elder to me... yeah, that was what I calculated mentally.
****

It was the sixth week since I started going to the bookstore; that guy who worked part time smiled at me when I entered which was unusual as he had never shown any interest in me before. By now Mr Danish knew me and I used to have some general conversation whenever I enter his bookstore. As he was the only one who seemed normal to me since the time I came to this new city.

I was searching for a book when to my surprise that guy came near and suggested me "The Great Gatsby".

"It's nice, you should read it," he said and went back to attend others.

"Thanks," I smiled.

That was the first time he spoke to me. He impressed me in some way as he wasn't one of those who stalk or who would see a beautiful girl and would hit on. I was getting curious about him but every time I thought that way his uninteresting looks made me clear that either he was a gay or he already had someone in his life. I noticed that many girls who visit the bookstore hit on him but he just smiles and courteously rejects their offer to hang out with them.

Why waste your energy to think about somebody who already belongs to someone? My inner conscious warned me.

****

One day after classes I thought of stopping by a restaurant as I was starving. I felt really bad and missed my friends as I hate eating alone. I went in, scanned the place; the environment was soothing. A family sitting on the left and a couple having their romantic conversation as the girl was blushing. I sat on the table next to that family and had a look at a menu.

"Hey," someone said.

I looked up, almost sure it wasn't for me. But I was surprised; it was the guy from the bookstore.

"Hey," I replied smilingly.

"Are you alone or expecting someone?" he asked.

"Alone," I replied, trying to believe I would have a company that also the one about whom I was curious.

"Do you mind if I join you?" he was courteous.

"Not at all," I welcomed his company.

"I am Kunaal," he finally introduced himself.

"Smira."

For the first time, I noticed he had dimples and his smile was breath taking which was rare to find. This was the first time I got to know him, he was working with an IT firm and as he also loved books, he was working on the weekend at the bookstore. He actually wanted to be a writer. We had snacks and a soothing conversation.

He is charming and well-mannered… I thought.

****

Next day I was actually excited as it was Sunday and I was going to see Kunaal again. I towards the bookstore, he smiled at me and I smiled back sheepishly. I had a conversation with Mr Danish and sat reading. I expected Kunaal would come to talk for a while but soon I realised he was quite professional. So, I started reading instead of letting my thoughts wonder about him. After a while, I realised Kunaal was there smiling at me.

"Let's go out and grab something to eat," he suggested.

I squinted at the watch, I didn't realise it was almost two hours I was engrossed in reading.

"Yeah," my stomach was growling.

He laughed at me and we headed to a nearby takeaway shop.

"Why are you always alone?" he asked grabbing a roll he ordered.

"Maybe these people don't like me," I said thoughtfully. He laughed.

"No seriously, these people are different. I tried to be friends with few in the coaching centre and but they are strangely hard to digest," I said thoughtfully.

"People are not different, they all are the same. You are unique," he corrected me.

No one had ever said it so beautifully, I thought.

This time, our conversation was deep, not about him or me but about life and for the first time in my life I had found someone with whom I could talk about anything, who used to think the way I did, and we were sharing the same wavelength. We could even discuss and talk on some topics that we didn't even agree at the same time.
*****

I was busy until next Sunday in preparing assignments, solving objective questions and trying out some coding. Classes were getting interesting as I was among the top five students and now these strange people had started coming to me for some help in finding out the answers but still I didn't have any real friend. I used to eagerly wait for Sunday as Kunaal would be there in the bookstore.

One Sunday, my batch mates surprisingly thought of going for a movie and that was a chance for me to hang out with them, to know them a bit better but going on a movie would mean that I wouldn't be able to see Kunaal.

It wasn't that I want to be in a relationship with him but it was just that I found him interesting, it was something I had never felt for someone else ever. After a lot of stress and hard work for a week, few hours around someone whose presence you adore wasn't a bad idea and wouldn't harm anyone... *I deserve it.*

I decided to stay in the bookstore for a while and would go for a movie and join them if I would be just staring him or reading alone but if he would be talking then I won't be going anywhere. As by now, I knew he wasn't an unprofessional person who would flirt while working and anyways he never flirted; I was the one whose strings were playing the fantasy.

****

Sunday, I put on the pain to dress well.

Unexpectedly he was standing nearby and his eyes twinkled when he saw me.

I smiled.

"Almost a week," he said.

"Yeah, it was a tiring week," I replied amazed by what he said.

"So, how is everything?" he walked with me towards the fiction corner which wasn't expected.

"It's all cool. How was your week?" I asked finally confirmed he really wanted to talk and he was happy to see me again.

"Work, work and more work," he laughed.

"I have completed the book that you suggested, what should I read next?"

"Quit reading for today, let's go out," he said confidently. "Only if you like," he added.

"This Kunaal is so free and frank but earlier it was always a wall between us", I was startled.

"Okay, relax don't take me wrong I am asking you because I actually had a good time when we last met. It has been after so long that I have met someone and I don't have to pretend for anything and yes I missed you since the time you said bye," he said it all in one go.

"Yeah, sure," I agreed as it was clear and could be seen in his eyes that he wasn't planning to harm me in any way.

"You are behaving strange, I could never imagine you would ask me out this way," I replied honestly.

"Does that amazes or disappoints you?" he asked with utmost sincerity in his tone.

I looked at him, my heart was changing its rhythm, "amaze, of course," I said.

We headed towards the restaurant we went to last time. We ordered food and then got back to know each other more.

After a while, my phone buzzed. It was from one of my batch mates from coaching. It was a reminder that I have to arrive at the movie if I want to make it on time.

"We all going to a movie, do you wanna join?" I asked him gathering some courage.

"I have some stuff that too is completed."

"Even I don't want to go," I sadly added as I wanted to be with him for some more time.

"C'mon, hang out with them and have fun. I Will see you next Sunday," he suggested.

"Okay," I replied.

"Wait, this is for you," he handed me a book which he was holding.

I thanked him and we bid our adieu.

Miss you already, I mumbled.

I was all into him, he wasn't a control freak, he values myspace and he was so courteous. I was so sure I was fallen for him head over heels. I was amazed reading the note he left for me in the book "Notebook" by Nicholas Spark and was glad to know the feelings were mutual.

Dying to take you in my arms;
To feel the warmth of your love,
To fill the emptiness of my heart,
To explore you more...
Far away from here on the planet of love, someday will be together,
Crossing the limits of my body that have trapped my soul,
You will be mine and I will be yours.
FOR YOU
MY LOST GIRL... who could be found in books?

I like you Simar
Kunaal

Speechless; as I was neither a poet nor somebody so good at expressing her feelings. But I was on cloud eleven actually. I ran my fingers over the words to feel as those words were for me. I got so cold out of nervousness, was having butterflies in my stomach. This wasn't a first time that someone told me he likes me but this was the first time I already liked the person who was saying this to me.

****

The next Sunday I went to the bookstore but he was not there, I asked Mr Danish about him but he was clueless. I was really sad as I waited for six days to meet him and completed all my study stuff so, this Sunday I could be all with him.

I waited the whole day and came back hopelessly. But that made me wonder about so many things as few more weeks were left and I would move on to a different city and would do the job. I kept my place and where I did coaching and where I hail from, all secret because if one percent Kunaal turns out different to what I thought he was, then I could easily get rid of him. He didn't know anything about me except that I do coaching somewhere and staying here for few more weeks.

I decided to take his number and dozed off wondering what future holds for us.

****

I managed to control my urge to see Kunaal till Wednesday but on Thursday I decided to take his information from Mr Danish and contact him as he would only turn up on Sunday. After coaching, I went straight to the bookstore. I took the details of Kunaal, Mr Danish smiled while handing the details and said, "Since he joined this place, you are the first girl he ever talked to. He is a nice guy."

I took an auto and went to his place as his number wasn't reachable. It was a weird feeling like what would he think of my sudden appearance but I shove away my doubts and headed towards the given address, finally, I was standing before the door. I was about to knock but noticed the door was open. I went in and after crossing the hall I heard someone. I could feel there was somebody; I was about to call his name but something caught my attention and I ran away from there.

He would never know I came there but what I saw just left me shattered into pieces. He was there with someone, their lips locked into each other.

It took me minutes to control my sobs, to actually digest what I saw; a chilled wave went through my spine.

He was betraying me.

****

After few more weeks, I completed my coaching and moved to Delhi. It was a strange kind of restlessness. I wanted to ask why he did that to me but quit the idea as he would have come with an excuse and I wouldn't be able to trust him again.

****

Betrayal left you nowhere, it shakes your belief, your faith, and you stop trusting people around you, you do lose your confidence. You build walls sealing yourself and your heart; you won't let anybody cross that because you don't want to get hurt again. You are no more what you used to be, you become a completely new you and trust me, it isn't a better version of yours. It's mostly the devil you search for in people, instead of searching for the angel because you have started thinking angel doesn't exist. You lose faith in the most beautiful, sacred sensation that God has gifted us, Love.

Day's were somehow easier but nights were harsh. At night you are alone, you don't have to pretend, and no one would come to distract; no noise of vehicles, gadgets, people... it's all peaceful out there and at home. Peace helps you connect to your soul and when your soul is injured, bleeding; it screams. At day the screams could be suppressed but at night it become audible and thus tears give the visibility to your pain. You let that salty water comes out of your eyes because no one is watching.

Like a warrior each day pretending I didn't give a damn but at night it was all over. and you become a pacifist. I put down the mask and lie down weeping.

Someone has said time heals every wound, after a year I got used to all this. I started attending parties, I had a group of friends who cared for me at the time I needed. I became tough enough to pretend that I had moved on to the world but no matter how strong we become we always wanted someone to kiss our wounds and would see those injuries as opportunities to fill in his love. We all want that someone whom we could show the hidden side of ours who cries when we fail, we all want somebody to be at our back as a strong pillar to help us stand again and would never let us give up.

I was living a life in which I had given up all my faith in love and I had stopped searching for that *someone* as my fairy tale ended up a year ago and that left me broken. I kept reading at night to kill my loneliness as nights still hasn't stopped haunting me.

****

After two years, I was in a bookstore looking to fetch something good to read and something caught my attention, a book named, "LOST GIRL."

It reminded me of Kunaal as he wrote it under his poem which I still had with me, *his only memory*. I took it and turn it around to know the author, it was him. A tear

70

came rolling down my cheeks, it was after two long years that I was seeing him.

I bought the book and read it. It was all about me, it was all what we talked, how we met. I was confused, *an illusion or reality*, I thought.

At the end, he wrote, "I am still waiting for you."

Am I thinking too much or it was just a mirage?

That night I slept hugging the book, I realised I was still in love with him, two years of effort that I had put into hate him and in forgetting him all went in vain and the truth was, I was just trying to run away pretending even to myself that I forgot him which actually never happened.

I searched online; Kunaal was coming to Delhi for a book launch I decided to meet him to ask if he still loves me then why he was with someone??

****

It was all crowded, people were actually crazy for him. He came after an hour and people were crazy to get a chance to have selfie and his autograph. He was just a few steps away from me. I was moving forward but a thought restrained my steps.

But what if he would think I am behind his fame, I came back because he is famous.

Kunaal would never understand I should not bother about him and his fake story. He used me as a character, he wanted fame he got; it has nothing to do with me.

I turned around but felt a hand on my shoulder, it was him. He grabbed me and took away from the crowd who was madly calling out his name.

"Why you left me, like that? Why you abandoned me?" he was actually angry.

I was looking at him bewildered.

"I need an answer, do you think that it's a joke, do you have any idea how much I tried to get to you. How hard it was to wait for two years to live dreaming about us to be together every night," he was holding me and I was just trying to believe that it was all happening for real.

I pushed him away, "Do you have any idea how hard it is to know that the person you are madly in love with, betrayed you?"

"Betrayed?" he looked at me confusingly.

I narrated everything I saw.

"Oh! Damn. She was my colleague who was behind me and she came suddenly over me and I pushed her away, I swear I love you, it was you about whom I thought every second of the time you left me," he held my hand.

"Why am I still here with you when so many girls are shouting my name out there?" he took me in his arms, kissed me gently and made me fall in love with him again, the entire grudge drained out in a second.

"You were the one I loved and I waited for you from the day you disappeared.

I love you my lost girl," he said trying to catch his breath.

Vama Gor

Vama Gor is a 17-year-old girl, with a flair for writing. She began writing at a tender age of 11. Since then, she has written a number of stories, poems, blogs, and plays . Apart from writing , she has a great interest in dancing , acting , swimming , cooking ,travelling and meeting new people .She has an affinity towards classical and western music .She describes herself as someone who was born to be on the stage , as performing arts runs through her veins . She blends in, her favourite subjects like History, Psychology and Economics, in her stories. She picks up inspiration from real life scenarios, as she feels – no event of life should be undermined!

Answers

"Daddy!" Aisha exclaimed, as she ran towards the door, with her little feet, to greet her father. "Hey, princess" he said as he lifted her up and hugged her.

This was a daily routine. Aniket would return from his job to see his children, run up towards the door to greet him. It was the most pure form of love - no conditions, no bonds.

"Where is your sister?" He asked the little girl, who very innocently caught his pinky finger, and took him to her room. Sanya was engrossed in her phone, smiling occasionally.

"Nobody cares if I am here," said her father, looking at her, mocking her instead. A voice emerging from the dreaded silence expect for the usual 'ping' of her messages, caught up her attention. "Dad!" she said and ran up to him.

Aniket had beautifully summed up his entire world in his family- his two daughters, and his wife. He lived for them, and earned for them. Moreover, his jolly and straightforward attitude made him his wife's trustworthy companion, and his 18 year old daughter's, best friend. Never did he hesitate to speak his heart out to either his wife, or his daughter. But being beautifully open minded, also he was soft hearted; a mysterious essence to his normal self. He had a strong, bold, lively and an ethically compassionate face that was wildly popular amongst people he knew. But deep within, Aniket was a different man. A man with a dominant emotional side. A man, who had the best control of his emotions. And a great understanding between the right and the wrong.

After having bath, the family sat down for dinner. Dinner was usually the time wherein the family would talk about the entire day's whereabouts. And also, there was a rule. That both the good and the bad experiences, shared by any family member, would have to be swallowed down into the belly, with the food.
So Sanya, always chose the time, to shock her parents.

"College was fun today. I loved the lecture on Art history. It was exciting. Also, the teacher is very interactive and funny. We call her Miss 'funny bones.' she said, adding a bit of drama. "Mother, do you know, I am her favourite pupil. She loves to give me extra information about different paintings, painters and writers all over the globe."

"That is exciting", said her mother, gulping the soup down her throat.

"Yes, mother. Also, she has given me the information of a few courses I can apply in, after High school. She has been my favourite teacher until now. I will miss her" she said, sighing.

"Where is she going?" said her mother, inquisitively, whereas her father listened to the conversation with keen interest. He had given Sanya the liberty to pursue whatever she wanted to.

"She is going away; to Delhi. Next month. She has got a job offer from a renowned university that will pay her much more than here in Mumbai. Also, she will be given the opportunity to pursue PhD in Art history." she said, with a smirk.

"If you really are interested in History, I will ask some of my colleagues for some good history tutor, with whom you can do a workshop, on art history."

Aniket was more than happy to know that his daughter was being focused towards her career when a message popped up on his phone.

It was an informal reminder of the open day, at Sanya's High school, that was at 11.30 am the next day. No wonder, she was flattering at dinner time, her father thought.

Dressed up in white, both the father and daughter, stood outside the classroom where the economics' professor was seated. Sanya had faired quite well in Economics and was in the list of the top ten rankers in her grade.

She seemed to do well in Psychology, English and Sociology, whereas her Hindi was a little weak. Stroking off each subject from her rough, she said: "Now, History".

"I remember, but is it necessary to visit every teacher? I know you are good at history" he said, looking at his watch.

"Dad, this is the most important," she said sternly.

Outside classroom 'XII C', was a huge queue. Many parents stood outside the room, waiting for their turn. June had already begun, but the scorching heat seemed to create a feeling of claustrophobia in the small aisle where they were waited long enough.

Finally Mr. Aniket was called in with Sanya . The history professor seemed to be in her forties, but yet had a glow on her face. Her hair, still were silky and full of life. Her skin was fair and she had a beautiful, comforting smile. She looked like an easy – going woman but with an aim in life.
Sanya sat down on the chair, where as her father stood until he had introduced himself to the teacher. She was standing near her cupboard, where she seemed to be finding Sanya's result.

"I must say I am very impressed with you Sany--" she stopped as soon as she exchanged looks with him.

"Sadhana?" he stammered in disbelief

"Aniket?" she said, petrified.

"Aniket!" she called out from the stand. "Aniket!" she shouted once more.

In the summer heat, with beads of sweat trickling down his face, Aniket stood motioning his co-player to pass him the ball. Positioned at the centre of the court he looked first at the ball, and made up a strategy of his own. No sooner the ball felt like a toy in his hand, as it flexibly dribbled its way till the where, he lifted up his arm, and took the shot. An easy win.

Not only was Aniket, the best basketball player in college but also someone for whom most of the girls fell for. And the girl he fell for, was Sadhana . Timid, shy and extremely beautiful.

It was a rainy day when Aniket had expressed his feelings for her. Both stood near the college campus; clothes drenched in rainwater, facing each other, where Aniket held a rose and Sadhana stood in awe. Definitely it was a clichè scene, but one thing seemed to make it different – two people in the rain, falling in love.

Five years of college life seemed to vanish away. They were more than happy to be together. They had been dating each other for 5 years now, and it seemed that they would be with each other for ever . They were the most inspirational couple in college.

"I think we should get married" Sadhana said, looking into Aniket's eyes. Whenever this topic came out, Aniket was unable to look her straight into her eyes. "We will, when the right time comes" he used to say. "Just imagine, you will go to work, while I will prepare good food for you, I will take care of children and also of our house. We will be with each other for life time" "Sadhana, this isn't you. You are meant for more. You don't have to take care of children.. You need to be independent and believe in yourself".

Time does fly. It was Sadhana's birthday.   June 28. Dressed up in his best clothes, with his best perfume, and the best gift, he landed up at Sadhana's house and rang the doorbell.

The school bell rang, breaking the connection of over a thousand memories. The clouds vanished from their heads, and they saw each other, face to face .

Facing reality.
"Mr Aniket , please take a seat," she said , putting up a smile that had mixed emotions. "S-So how are—'' he fumbled. "So how is she doing? Well well, very well. She seems to be very much interested in Art History, Aniket .. ji" she finished, correcting her sentence. "Thank you So Much," he said, shaking hands with her, while Sanya left. He quietly saw her leave the room and waited.

 "How are you here?" he asked, wanting more answers then he could contain. "I have been working here Aniket

. I understand you are thrilled. So am I, it is not the perfect time to speak now." "Here is my card," he said, removing a card from his chest pocket and placing it on the table.

His legs felt it impossible to move, they had been rooted into the ground, but the mind did the movement and got him till the car outside her High School.

Six days that the encounter had taken place. And then suddenly between meetings, came a call. Unknown Number.

"Hey," the voice said. He recognised instantly. "Hello", he said, holding his horses.
"Why not meet up for coffee today?" she asked hesitantly. "yeah sure, Crimson Café , 5 pm".

She looked beautiful with the white *kurti* that she had on. Her hair was left open, with streaks of brown. Her metallic earrings, danced its way while she herself walked down to the café. Looking around she spotted Aniket, sitting uneasily at a corner of the café.

"Hey," he said, as she came towards him. They gave each other a formal greeting and sat down, talking about the exact reason why they had decided to meet.

"28th June 1994, Monday 10 am, I stood outside your house, ringing your bell, for 2 hours. I slept at your doorstep the entire night, just to know, that you had gone. What was that, that you couldn't tell me? What was the reason, you never looked back?" he asked, eyes welling up.

She pursued her lips. Occasional chills went down her spine. She had to tell him. She had no choice.

"27th June, a day before my birthday, something unexpected happened. Something that I never imagined of" she said, reimagining every moment.

"At midnight, I heard a gunshot. I was in my room half-asleep. I ran up to my drawing room to see the corpse of my mother on the floor. The carpet, soaking endless blood, and a man in a white shirt standing with a bullet in his hand, his eyes looked miserable, his face tired." she said , quite mechanically , but remembering every detail of the scene.

"What?" his jaw dropped open. "Next morning, I found my father, hanging from the fan.'' "What happened? Make it clear". "My aunt and I visited a psychiatrist with my father. His unusual behaviour was misleading us since a long time. We got to know, he was suffering from schizophrenia. Now, it was clear, who kept knives in his room, who finished all the sleeping pills."

Aniket was in a state of shock. Such events were not even imaginable.

"Mother was speaking to dad about some bills that had to be paid. Never did I know that something like this would happen." she gasped. "So do you mean to say, your father –'' "My father killed her." Answers were now coming into the picture. The dust over their chapter was clearing away.

"Luckily my aunt was there with me and she decided to take me away to Bengaluru with her. I tried contacting you since then, but there I had a different life, struggles and suffering. Then I returned to Mumbai after 7 years and tried going to your old house. Vacant. "Yes, I shifted," he said, with a hint of guilt.

"I tried contacting you. I had none of our friend's numbers. And then I heard that you were a married man with a child. I was happy for you." Both sat in utter silence and shock.

"You know Aniket, maybe now I have understood, that we were not meant for each other. After so many years, it's strange, but I don't feel the way I used to feel before, for a moment at school the other day, I thought I fell in love again" she said, hoping she didn't hurt him.

"Actually, the feeling is mutual" he said, thinking of why this was happening.
"We are here today because of our destiny. We were not meant to meet each other, to fall in love again. But the times that we spent together made us want more. Our love was pure until it existed. Maybe for those 6 days I

was falling in love with you, again. This is the real essence of love. But here, today we meet, to say some unspoken words, we failed to say back then" he said, smiling.

"I always thought, that I would tell this to you someday", Aniket said. "Thank you" he continued "Thank you for coming in my life, and making me compassionate, calm and understanding," he said with truthfulness in his eyes.
"Thank you for coming in my life. You inspired me to become independent, you made me who I am today," she said.

"I will always have respect for you in my heart'' he said.
"So will I" she smiled.
 "I don't know if i will ever see you again, I am going to Delhi. But the world is round, and the some or the other day are heads are going to clash", she smirked as she sat in her car. He waited there until she had disappeared into the mists. His eyes remained open, for a long while. The truth was difficult to digest. Rain poured over him. The first rain of the season had arrived. Words hit his ears like a lightning bolt. His hands trembled in uncertainty. Isn't it true that we learn so much from people who come in our lives and seep through our minds? Such people are like the cool breeze that calm our innards, giving us inner peace and strength. Karma does exist and gets back to you, one day in life. Even the leaden heart melts down to warm up our bodies. Life has a surprise of unexpected twists and turns, events that

change it completely. What we have come down on the planet is - to question our reasoning and to get answers. And when the time comes, god gives those answers to us.

The body is just a mortal piece of lust, desire and expectations, which degrades slowly and gradually perishes. There are in life, a few important questions that we must ask ourselves. Who are we? And what is the cause and motive of our existence?

The day we find the answer to these questions, life won't remain the same. Life will become a less complicated place, giving you the answer to almost every question. But do these fascinating questions evoke the divine presence within the mortals?

The answer is - No. These questions make us realize the reason why we are on this earth and the designated task we have to accomplish. It is strange that we don't even realize when we may just learn important lessons of life. It is strange that a few incidents can change your thinking processes, your vision, the way you see the world. Sometimes when we feel things are falling apart, they actually are falling in place. But the human brain, rather than understanding the evident truth, goes into the mode of depression, anger, sadness and frustration.

When life was in turmoil, god came down to sort matters between these two angels. Angels who understood the meaning of life. A life that threw them down. Down, deep within the pit of frustrations. But they stood up, standing out of the common mortals. They became uncommon and they found something, that we all are seeking – The Answer.

Shilpa Dhar

Born in Srinagar, Kashmir valley Shilpa has seen the insanity of humans at a very early stage in her life. She was just three when her house was burnt down by terrorist, post which her family left the valley. She says she indeed misses her motherland a lot. This is one of the major reasons why she writes.

Shilpa has done her schooling from Dehradun and Jammu followed by perusing B-Tech in IT from Chandigarh.

She has also worked with 3 Punjabi Feature Films and done a show with Disney Channel for Kids. Writing and acting both are her food for life !!

She Quotes "When we act we are most of the time not being ourselves or doing the role what we really want to from within but when I write I am always happily doing what's storming in me to come out and flow through my ink."

Her family is her strength. Its the unconditional love that germinates a blossoming flower in her spreading its fragrance.

She also quotes, "I owe my whole life to Sai baba."

"The Magic Woman"

He would come to her often, but this time, he looked little anxious. "Can we please have another quick session on my new investment pattern?" His voice had faith, a faith she had been looking for ages. She was one of the most famous tarot card readers in the town. People from all walks came to her. Her eyes dazzled, like always as he sat in front of her for consultation. She smiled and the blue sapphire stone was sparkling brightly on her hands as she swiftly shuffled the deck of 78 cards to unwind the secrets of this man in front of him.

In his middle thirties, David would always come in her compound; peep in like a small child, with a face full of questions and doubts. She as a norm would welcome him with a serene look and the most beautiful curvy smile.

"The VIII of wands shows me a sudden change in your investment pattern, which would fetch you a complete world. The world you always longed for." David felt calm. "Can I say something to you?" he said.
"Go ahead".
"You are a MAGIC WOMAN." The room was dark, big white glaze of the candle at the centre of the table sparkled brightly through her eyes as she laughed at his words.

David and Caira; the magic woman had met a few months back. Ever since then David rushed to her for every small decision of his life and she loved reading him. "Coffee?" asked Caira. "Well, not really fond off", said David. She was getting fond of him, though. "Magic woman, every time I come to you, you don't take the fees from me and keep it pending. May I know when I am supposed to clear all your debts?" he asked.

She laughed, her vibrant laugh echoed through the bright orange curtains of her room. "You would clear them all when the TIME comes." She said with the spark in her eyes, her laughter had music; she was in love with him. It was evident from the wait in her eyes. But, however, mystic she appeared to the people she could not read the other side of him. Months passed by and it was almost a year now and Caira decided to tell him how much she loved him. She wanted to tell him how much she wanted to be a part of his every dilemma, every setback and be a spiritual soul mate support to him.

"Have you seen the small cute puppy sitting beneath the mango tree?" She asked. "Yeah, it's hot out there. What a relief to the poor chap!" David said. "Yes!! That's the relief I get when you are around. It's like I am away from all the sun burns one could ever get", her eyes spoke with her tongue. "I feel so protected", she added.

The room filled with silence. David laughed. His laughter broke the silence, hahaha, "Protected! The magic woman feels protected. You must be kidding me." "What makes you laugh?" she questioned. "This is so funny. The damsel is in need of protection", he laughed louder. His laugh pierced her only heart. Probably, her only love apart from the morning birds, the chanting mantras and now this man had come to an end.

She could have never explained to him what she held in her heart and he could never read her eyes. As they say, not everyone can be a good reader. "Time for transformation." Her teacher had once told her.

"It's again ace of pentacles. Congrats! A lot of money coming your way", she said as she read his cards, cards that spoke to her and understood her more than the man in front of her. Two days passed by!! Friday morning David rang her bell. He had cracked a deal. His fingers kept pressing the bell button. The door was opened by a young girl. He rushed in and found Caira's session room door ajar.

"Caira Caira", he shouted. Caira's coffee mug was placed on her wooden table. The Buddha she worshipped smiled at him. David shouted her name again. "Caira has gone." The young girl said while offering him a glass of water. "Gone where?" he asked. "She's gone to the hills. No one knows where the hills where she went are." "Jesus!" he cried.

He left. It was hot. Sun shone brightly. He saw the puppy sitting below the tree seeking its shade. He wanted a similar shade. Perhaps, that's what Caira meant. He kept trying her number but in vain!!!

"Sam, I need your help."He called up a friend who was an in-charge of the local police." I need a number to be traced up. I just lost someone." "Well, how urgent is that?" he asked. "Even before I breathe the next breath!!" Dave said. "The number last worked at the foothills of Atlantope," Sam informed.

Next morning, David was standing at the foothills of Atlantope. There were hardly any people around. He saw a monastery. There was no trace of Caira in the entire periphery covering the monastery. It started raining!! There was so much he wanted to ask her. But there were no cards. There was no Caira!! "Young man what are you looking for"? An old voice called from behind. "Well, I am looking for my life. I just lost her." "Well, if she's your life how can you lose her?" the old man questioned. "Will you help me find her?" he begged. "Well, it's your journey. Your manifestation will lead you to her. Have the conviction that you still have her. It's the faith that matters." Days passed by. He could not find her. They had seen the whole area only the forest was left.

"Why in the world would she be there?" He asked the old man who apparently stayed with him till now. "Maybe she's different or maybe she's a beast." He winked to add humour. The birds flocked by. The trees paved their way into the jungle. David could hear the gushing of the brook. He remembered Caira once said she loved that sound.

"Let's drink some water."He bent to fulfil his quench. The quench indeed was fulfilled!! His eyes met the wavy eyes reflected in the pristine water. It was she sitting across the brook with closed eyes as pure as the fresh morning light. He felt like crossing the river and shouting her name. There was a similar gushing inside him like the gushing of the brook. The old man gave a no signal. They took a long route and reached the other side. He whispered her name in her ears "Caira".

She opened her eyes. For the first time, David saw her eyes speak and could read them flawlessly. They read. "I knew you would come." "Can I please protect you from the animals and take you away from this dense jungle?" "You were right one day I would clear all your debts. Who knew it would happen amidst a jungle."
She laughed. This time, her laughter echoed through the tall trees of the jungle.

And yes!!! The reason for her laughter was justified...He would come to her often...But this time; he had come just for her...

Heena Joshi

Born in Ajmer, raised in a small district Bhilwara, Heena completed her schooling and then gave a whirl to journalism degree. She entered into journalism with the common dream of being on TV but soon realized that she had her heart and soul in writing. She completed her masters in Journalism and Mass Communication and took teaching as full-time career for sometime. She has worked as a freelancer with renowned dailies like The Times of India and Hindustan Times. Travelling, reading, writing and spending time with family work like meditation to her.

A Missed Call from Life

We met for a reason; either you are a blessing or a lesson. "Ma'am,you will be sitting in the section on the first floor from Monday, right?" to which Tamanna nodded affirmatively while signing out of biometric authenticator on the first floor. With the wafting wooden fragrance in the air, Armaan on the first floor felt compelled to take a peek in the corridor. There she was, silky light brown open tresses playing hide and seek on her confident face and natural pink lips. Her unsuccessful efforts of putting those beautiful golden strands back were mesmerising. Her long yet loose peach colour shirt was poetry to her slender guitar shaped built. He took a deep breath again and appreciated the beauty. His eyes followed her while wrapping up his desk to call it a day at work. Within a span of minutes, he was downstairs and his eyes could not stop searching her. He could not see her, but the fragrance made a permanent residence in his heart and mind.

People enter your life through many doors (mediums) and she did enter his life through the office door. They met in the office where he first laid his eyes on her. Little did they both know what fate had in store for them.

Monday morning seemed brighter when he entered the office and saw the fragrance queen sitting adjacent to her seat. Though the seat arrangement made her sit keeping her back at his seat, but he felt happy without knowing why.

"Tamanna, he is Armaan and he will be guiding you for your work here," said the potbellied, petite man while munching his burger, she was bound to call him boss. Armaan got up on instructions and dragged a chair beside her. She was clad in a purple sleeveless kurti, her hair fell loose on her milky white arms and her beautiful black eyes had a faded tinge of kohl. He couldn't take his eyes off those kohl laden eyes transfixed on the computer screen to understand the intricacies of the job profile. She was nodding in attention. Her blank eyes and stern look made her look more mysterious to him.

There was an internal LAN networking system to communicate with office colleagues to make it hassle free communication on various floors. A pop up from Tamanna came first, "Armaan, Independence day is round the corner, should we plan some offers?" He replied, "Wait, I will come there and show you what kind of offers we have launched before."

The day came to an end at work and that is when he witnessed the newbie all lost in her world with the earphones plugged in. He instantly opened his chat window and pinged her, "All work and no play, makes Jack a dull boy. Not bored with these earphones the whole day?" "I have music to listen to." She replied. "I did not know that songs talk too", came Armaan's witty reply which was responded with just a grinning smiley. "I love the lyrics and I try to use them in my writing." Armaan got impressed and typed further, "Oh so the busy bee writes too? I wish I can get a note dedicated to me written by you. Just kidding." Little did they know that the wish was granted. Little did Tamanna know that she would be the medium of fulfilling his wish.

A week passed and it was next Monday again. Before Armaan could think of why, he caught himself sending her, "So ma'am, how was your weekend?" "Hey, I spent the Sunday eve with friends and we made some foreign chicks our friends during a TDS (truth, dare or situation game)," was the reply of Tamanna. "Oh, foreign chicks! Wish I was so lucky," Armaan replied with a winking smiley. "Oh sure, why don't you join us someday?" Tamanna said. This was the beginning of their beginning. Time flew, conversations increased, numbers got exchanged and finally the day came for an unofficial rendezvous. Drizzling gave the evening a romantic, dramatic and special touch to make them special. It felt like the whole universe was conspiring to bring them together. Few meets, long walks, many talks and serene eye locks did the trick. Rains were icing on the cake. They were head over heels before they could realise. They got addicted of each other's company, started speaking each other's mind before letting the other speak. Such was the soul connection.

Tamanna who had a flair for writing and never left any stone unturned to celebrate moments in her life with words, wrote Armaan, the first dedication through words: Happiness knocks your door when you are too hopeless to smile. That is when the love of my life...you knocked the door of my heart n brought back my smile. Our steps taken together towards our destination may have their own challenges but your company always nourished courage and joy in me. Your love resurrected my broken belief in people and the world doesn't seem bad anymore to me. This time, its ecstasy evolving while I am writing this note to you finally handing over my heart to you with these words. I want you to move ahead and take a walk unknown with me but my soul has a deep bruise which I never told you before. I promise I will tell you soon. Many emotions surging up. Amidst all this harmony of emotions. I'm waiting for your response. To take another step to seal our bond with more memories. I am walking on a path of roses where I can foresee us sharing the goods and bads of life forever Armaan. I love you and waiting for your response.

Armaan replied: I am in the world of pleasure which I never felt before. Cloud nine seems to be an understatement while expressing what I am feeling right now. Tamanna you are my dream girl and swept me off my feet by surprising me before I could do. I love you too regardless of whatever it is which you want to tell me. If you feel it is important to share please do else I would not want you to share at the cost of your comfort. I will soon talk to our parents about us.

It was the beginning of the journey unseen, unfelt or may be unexpected. With the whirlwind of love cascading all around, Tamanna was captured in the spell of Armaan and writing was put on backburner before she could realise.

Every relationship has its secrets, so did this one too. After spending a romantic weekend in a movie theatre with Armaan, she suddenly uttered with a serious note, "There is something about me which you don't know and I want to tell you!" Her declaration etched a smile on

Armaan's face and he comforted her by holding hands and said, "I remember you mentioning it before in your writing. Take your time; I am always there to listen."

Days passed and Armaan once meekly reminded Tamanna in fun to reveal that secret the very next day, which all of a sudden, made her heartbeats racing and throat parched. Armaan was too patient and very strong-willed to listen to anything but never thought to lose her. Next sun rose and also did set, it was confrontation time. Armaan was mature enough for not jumping to the topic and suggested a stroll with an ice cream feast. They found themselves sitting in the garden and he could feel the seriousness in her eyes but was not able to figure out the dampness in them. The realisation struck with the shock of seeing the droplets of tears in her eyes and sobs from her. He immediately pacified his princess as he could not see tears in her eyes; even if he had to put his everything on stake to protect them, he would. The confrontation was postponed for the next day as he wanted a place to hug her assuming the glum situation in the garden.

Armaan managed to arrange for a place which was his friend's flat for an hour and picked up Tamanna from her home. He could gauge the gravity of the situation yesterday when he witnessed her sobbing before revealing what she wanted to. He knew that there were chances of her breaking down and that would have called for uncalled attention in public places. They were in front of each other on the balcony. Roaring traffic was dwindled down in decibels and was outshined by 'kabhi alvida na kehna' song in the background in some shop downstairs. Both were silent and Armaan couldn't stop looking at the serene but sad beauty, whom he used to call his girl; his soul mate.

She entwined her hand in his before speaking and looked into his eyes. The vision was blurred with tears flooding her eyes but she gulped the lump in her throat and said, "Armaan, I am a rape victim. I was raped before two years while returning back from my call centre job. Since there were three people, I could not unmask them under their force. The case was reported but my family suggested of withdrawal of FIR due to the fear of bad name. I was broken and shattered for a year and tried to end my life. My family stood firm by me and that is how I managed to come out of the trauma. I also had to take professional help to sideline the horrendous incident in my memories. You helped in healing me with your sacred love, care and respect which resurrected my faith in loving the life again. I did not tell you before not because I was scared, but I wanted both of us to be sure about our future beforehand."

Their relationship had always needed fewer words, more eye locks; more of silences and no explanations. It had been more of a silent talk where they both understood what was on the others' mind. Armaan stood stupefied for few minutes which troubled Tamanna and she brought him back from his trance by tapping his shoulder. "Armaan, are you ok?" Armaan suggested for a walk towards home without uttering any more words. Tamanna knew he needed time to get adjusted to what transpired. The walk which they took back to her apartment to drop her back was the most tranquil yet stormy, most known since they had walked miles together as quality time yet there was an untold hurricane swirling up in his mind. "Have you already talk to your parents about us?" He finally asked before dropping her to her PG. "Yes love, they are not in favour as of now due to the typical caste objections but I am sure we will tread through gradually." Tamanna's assurance scared Armaan for the first time.

The next day he unfolded a 'possible bad news' by revealing that his mother was on bride hunt suddenly and they have a family to visit them for matrimonial purposes. It began raining heavily signifying the journey of a broken, bruised and raped heart. Yes, Tamanna felt raped again, this time, she was raped of emotions in love. She did not need more to talk or clarify as she understood once again without words. It was time to say Alvida (goodbye). She dropped the call and never picked another call from him. She sent him a text, "Have a good life ahead Armaan. My love for you will stay intact. I hope you stand by the one who comes next in your life. I don't have any grudges against you. Loving you was my decision where I did not put any condition of you loving me back the same way. I know it is tough to accept the raped girl as wife in front of your family. Convincing about caste is something else and convincing about a raped girl to marry with is a tough challenge to conquer. I wish you peace in life."

Her diary entry was: There was a lake. An ocean of joy and There was a river of tears. They had same dreams but different lives. A dream to move and an aim to flow. Little did they know that they would get a chance to intersect each other. To merge their sorrows and joys, to laugh in tears and to cry in joy. Like water, they submerged themselves to the twists n turns of life...and reached a point where they found NOTHINGNESS.

She went out and kept walking in the rain for almost three hours. The downpour never stopped and neither did she. Her head felt giddy against the cold which captured her body and stabbed heart and the world went bleak in next moment.

Tamanna opened her eyes to the green and white coloured walls. These walls of the hospital she feared since childhood but was gradually getting accustomed to. Her last stay in hospital was after the rape which added more dread to her frightful frame of mind. She could hear her mother talking to the doctor, "We were informed by some girl who found Tamanna lying fainted on the road. She claimed to have got our number from Tamanna's mobile which was working as it was waterproof. I hope nothing is serious about her getting unconscious. Also if you could manage to make us see that saviour girl if possible." The doctor broke the news in reply, "So far the tests have told us that she is suffering from pneumonia due to constantly getting drenched in rains. She is also under acute depression which would affect the speed of her recovery. The disease can get worst if your daughter gives up fighting willingly against it. Just medicines don't work if the patient gives up. As far as meeting with that saviour is concerned, she never returned back after calling you, bringing her here and doing the formalities. You can meet her only if she comes to meet the patient again. She did not leave any address to be contacted."

Her mother's sobs and her fathers' efforts to try to console her fell deaf on her mind for the moment. She did not want to live anymore. She was a disgrace to her parents. She brought them pain and shame with news of being raped and now this heartbreak was something she could not take anymore. She would not cause them more agony and would sneak out of the hospital and will go someplace where she was distant not only from her home, family and memories but also from her own self. She kept pretending asleep and just then entered Megha, her saviour with a bouquet.

She got to know that Megha was an independent girl who lost her parents in Tsunami and was living with one of her cousin brothers. Both of them somehow survived out of that fateful disaster and made it back the life with a bang. Megha was a journalist in The India Times newspaper for lifestyle and education section. The night when she found Tamanna was when she was returning back from a press conference in her Alto and brought Tamanna to the hospital on grounds of humanity. It was the beginning of a new friendship and new bond. It was also the hope for Tamanna's parents who left the city after a month of Tamanna getting healed. Since she was not ready to leave the city where she began her professional life, parents suggested her a change of job. Tamanna applied in the same newspaper where Megha was working and easily made it due to her writing skills.

Though Tamanna got a new job and shifted with Megha in an apartment. Her heart never revived back and she kept on ignoring meets with parents on festivals or in general. She was too embarrassed to face them despite their efforts.

A year crawled and one day Tamanna caught Megha once while crying secretly in the corner of their shared flat. That moment brought out the harsh reality in front of her. Megha who always sounded so chirpy and bubbly had a tough life not just because her parents were no more but also due to the shock being molested by the only family she claimed to have: Her cousin brother. He kept doing the nasty stuff to her until 5 years and she finally managed to run when she accidently found her parents' bank passbook where they had saved money for Megha. She immediately applied to newspaper and bought Alto for herself saying that it was company funded. She made an excuse of some meeting that night and left the city. Shockingly her brother never cared to trace her. She kept the courage and came to Jaipur where she began her new life. Megha broke down inconsolably for the first time. She was a brazenly bold girl and crying was not her cup of tea. Tamanna's heartbreak seemed so shallow when she heard the soul wrenching story of Megha. The incident shook Tamanna's spirit and it dawned on her that everybody has a pain to suffer in life. The challenge is to combat it and come out with a smile.

Realisations struck when you least expect them. It was Tamanna's time for realisation; those necessary realisations which were important for her survival. While consoling Megha when she broke down, Tamanna wondered on her power of hug which infused positivity in Megha. How could a love deprived person instil peace in Megha? Realisation said that both of them had missed all these moments of love in friendship. Tamanna ignored every moment to cherish with anyone else but Armaan during her relationship whereas Megha was yearning to get those deprived moments.

She realised that they both had missed the essence of life, celebrating festivals with loved ones- a precious time which Tamanna could gift to her parents if she had smiled. She missed those bonds which were always on toes to embrace her whereas she was lost with embarrassment and guilt in her own world since a year. She ignored their efforts and put them down; smashed them under her feet and still they all were there, standing strong for her in her thick and thin. All she needed was to turn back and see what all she turned a blind eye and a deaf ear to. This was not it, she was missing on the most important thing in her life: writing. Her diary was lying clad in layers of dust and the last entry she saw entered was when Armaan accepted her love. She felt numb on keeping her passion on the backburner for Armaan. Loving someone was not a fault but leaving everything to love someone definitely was one. She left the life she loved when she first fell in love.

Introspection led her to exploration and imbibed observation which made her look towards her parents whom she was overlooking since last one year. She saw the sadness in their eyes were suddenly wearier than they ever could be; maybe because of ceaseless trials of cheering her up. Life kept on calling her with open arms, but she never picked it up. It was a missed call from life which brought her back to her own life which was not lived. The missed call was in the form of Megha's soul-strangling story and her unbeatable courage to revive back.

Tamanna fell in love again, this time with her life unlived and the life which she unloved for some time. She fell in love with the people who loved her back, who respected her back and who accepted her as she was. She discovered herself when she lost herself once.

Her entry after a long time in the diary was: While wandering and mapping the empty streets, I saw one lamp post at the left fence. The emptiness and eeriness outside was absolutely complementing to my inner self. But there was still no peace. That lamp post seemed like a lonely soul. Standing all alone and sulking on the fact that everyone overlooked it, despite it lightening many worlds.

I went close and wondered that I too never acknowledged its presence before. It had withered in years and I remember I once bumped into it while playing n running. My head hit it and I can recall my curse saying, "You will die as you hit me."

A surge of emotions shivered me whether that curse was the reason of its anonymous yet vital presence here. I caressed it... it seemed as if it got scared. I gazed and wondered for how many years it faced this anonymity which eventually became a routine. The routine which was never wanted yet accepted forcefully. I kept on staring at it....

The next moment I found myself smiling with tears in my eyes and I discovered peace.

Diksha Sharma

Diksha Sharma, residing at Greater Noida, has successfully completed her graduation in Clinical Science from University of Oxford, London, United Kingdom and is currently working with Roshan Hospital. She is fond of literature and believes in penning her emotions. She believes in experimenting new and creative things.
Diksha Blogs at "The Rising Channels": http://therisingchannels.com

When you appreciated me for being a good young lady in front of others and always blessed me with your flawless Smile and glowing eyes.
Dedicated to you Grandma

A Love Relationship

It was a glorious morning at the home of Rhea & Karan, a brother-sister who belonged to a very rich family. Rhea was most loved by her father; she was a simple, frank and outgoing girl. Her hobbies included reading, travelling and music whereas Karan was his mother's heartbeat, he was reserved yet very simple and his hobbies included reading and playing the piano.

They were very close to each other & every secret of their lives was known to each other.
Their mother, Mrs Ahuja was a homemaker and a very affectionate mother; she loved to spend time with Rhea & Karan whereas their father Mr Ahuja was a businessman having a much-expanded website developing business so, he was a much busy person.
Karan and Rhea loved and respected their Parents unconditionally, though Karan hated his father because of his less availability to his family due to work. Rhea was pursuing her graduation from Delhi University in Humanities & Karan was pursuing his Master's in English Literature from Delhi University.

Karan always spent half of his time with Rhea & his mother or by playing piano in his room.
It was the day of college fest, Karan was the part of Orchestra in a drama and at the same moment, he saw a girl who was pretty enough to make Karan's sight fix on her. She was very simple but attractive and playing the

violin. Karan got hugely attracted towards her from the very first moment he saw her. For the first time, he felt so attracted to someone.

After their drama finished, Karan approached her and greeted, "You played the violin beautifully."

She responded with a smile, "Thank You! For appreciation, even you were amazing at the piano. I saw you were completely lost in it while playing, it was very intense and heart wrenching. By the way, what's your name?"

Karan replied, "My pleasure & Thank you too for appreciating me as I got this type of appreciation for the first time. I am Karan Ahuja and I am getting masters in English literature from Delhi University. What about you?"

She replied in a splendid way, "I am Kriya Arora. I'm pursuing my Master's in Economics from Delhi University itself"

The conversation went on and they were looking quite comfortable with each other. After sharing basic information they exchanged their cell numbers and waved bye to each other.
Karan was extremely happy as he found the pretty girl today. He shared this incident with his mom and Rhea; they too were fascinated while hearing that. Rhea started

teasing Karan and he blushed a bit. His mother hugged him and from back Rhea joined to complete family hug.
In next many days, Karan & Kriya started spending their leisure time together in either cafes or university campus.

After several months, Karan approached Kriya and in a shy manner told his feeling to her, he proposed her, "Kriya, you are the very first girl with whom I feel completely myself and with you, I can spend each and every second of my life. I have fallen in love with you Kriya. I love you very much and will take care of you every second. Do you love me? Will you accept me as your Partner? Will you give me the chance to pamper you every now and then? Will you allow me to love you in the way no one did to you ever?"

Charm was all over Kriya, she felt overwhelmed. She replied with a broad smile on her face, "I love you too Karan. You are the first guy in my life with whom I feel complete and on whom I trust for everything. Yes, I do accept you as my partner."

Then Karan embraced her in his arms and kissed her forehead as a promise to be with her until his last breath.
When Karan reached home, Mr. Ahuja met him in the living room and asked him casually about his college and life to which Karan replied rudely, "I'm good and doing great at college. I can take care of myself on my own".

After saying this, he went to his room & started playing the piano.

Mr Ahuja was sitting along with his wife and was blaming himself for everything and cried in front of his wife, Mrs Ahuja told him, "Honey! Be calm, everything will be all right." And further told him "Honey try to spend some time with Karan"

To which Mr Ahuja responded, "Okay! I'll try to spend some time with him."

Rhea was listening to the conversation and got disheartened and made herself determined to end this hatred relationship between his brother and father.

Next day was Sunday, so Karan decided to take Rhea to some café so that she can meet Kriya and become her friend as he wanted Rhea to be Kriya's friend too. He wants both the girls to have a good bond.

He went to Rhea's room and asked, "Rhea! Are you free today?"

Rhea replied, "Are you planning something?"

Karan told her, "Get ready. I'm waiting for you downstairs in the car. We are going to meet Kriya today at a café."

Rhea replies excitedly, "Okay I'll be there in a few minutes".

Karan left and went to inform his mother about the day & then took his car keys and went to the garage & started his car. He reached the front gate of their house where Rhea was waiting.

Rhea sat beside her brother and he started driving, on the way she asked her brother, "Why you hate daddy so much?"

Karan replied in a sad manner, "Rhea I don't hate him, I love him very much but you are aware of the fact that he never gave us time & also was never interested in knowing our lives so I get aggressive when I see him".

Rhea told him, "It is good to know that you love him, you're right that he didn't give us time much as he was doing pretty hard work so that he can give us all luxurious services, good education, food, clothes and tons of happiness. All he does is for making our future brighter."

And Rhea further requested her brother, "Please spend some time with him as I Know daddy misses you very much and you both have desires to talk to each other in your hearts."

Karan stopped car & replied further, "Okay Rhea! I will. Now let us go inside the café; she must be waiting for us." They reached inside the café and Karan saw Kriya and greeted her. They reached the table and sat with her. Karan introduced both of them to each other and left to give an order of coffee and some snacks. Riya and Kriya got indulged in some light chat and both were enjoying each other's company. Kriya appreciated Rhea's beauty and smile to which Rhea also appreciated her simplicity and pretty looks. All of the sudden Rhea asked, "Would you like to meet our family?" Kriya replied, "Yes, of course, I would love to." Rhea further asked, "Will you come with us today?" As I know my dad and mom are going to like you very much." Kriya said excitedly, "Yeah sure!" Rhea said, "Okay then, we will going to our home and have our lunch together."

Karan came back to the table along with coffee and snacks in his hand and sat. And Rhea asked Karan "Can we take Kriya to home for lunch?" Karan was surprised and replied, "Yes sure. We can but ask Kriya about it." Rhea told him," she is ready to come with us for lunch." Karan told Rhea to ask and inform mom about them, Rhea picked out her cell phone from the pocket and called her mother, she asked, "Mom can we bring Kriya di to our home for lunch?" Mrs Ahuja replied, "Yeah sure Rhea, you can as I and your dad are dying to meet her." Then Rhea replied, "Okay mom Thank you. Love you, mom." And Rhea disconnected the call, she told Karan the same. They finished their snacks and coffee, left for their home,

On the way back to home, they were talking about each other's lives and Rhea told her about their Parents and asked Kriya about her family. To which Kriya replied, "My dad is presently in the USA for some work and my Mom is a home maker. I am the only daughter of my Parents. I love my mom dad very much." Rhea asked Kriya "When will we get a chance to meet your family?" Kriya replied," As soon as my dad gets back at home, as I have already told them about Karan." Rhea happily said, "Wow! That's great. Karan bhaiya & I will be glad to meet your family."

They reached home; Mrs Ahuja was waiting for them along with Mr Ahuja. They got out of the car and Kriya greeted Mrs Ahuja & Mr Ahuja and asked about their health. After that, Rhea took her mom and Kriya to the kitchen to have some private time together and leaving Karan and Mr Ahuja in a living room.

Mr Ahuja liked Kriya, so he asked Karan, "Son, Do you love her?" Karan replied in a generous way, "Yes Dad. I love her and want to marry her." Mr Ahuja felt thoughtful, so further said, "Son. You've my permission to marry her." Karan for the first time smiled in front of his dad and apologised for the rude behaviour that he did in the past. In return, Mr Ahuja hugged his son and said, "Karan, I love you all. I always keep pictures of you, Rhea and you mom on my laptop, so that whenever I am not with you guys, I can at least see your photos and love you more. And I'm very sorry that I haven't given you much time." Karan replied, "Dad I'm sorry too that I always thought wrong about you."

Suddenly, Rhea came in the living room and hugged her father first and then whispered in Karan's ears," See I told you". Mrs Ahuja along with Kriya was standing and Mrs Ahuja got emotional and told Kriya that Karan & his father regained their relationship after a very long time. Upon hearing this, Kriya's eyes too got filled with tears.

Then they had lunch in a happily way, after lunch, Mr Ahuja asked Kriya, "Will you marry my son?" Kriya shyly replied, "Yes Uncle I will and will going to keep him and you all happy." Rhea hugged Kriya, Mr. & Mrs Ahuja gave their blessings to Kriya.

Karan told Kriya that "Let me drop you at your home." Kriya agreed and they both left for her home. On the way, Kriya told her plans about marriage and she told Karan that she will have the best husband in the world, they blushed together.

He dropped her home and came back to his home. They all celebrated the new love relationship of Karan and his father along with the celebrations of Karan's marriage to his girlfriend.

After a month, on 9 April 2014, Karan and Kriya completed their Master's and on the same day, Karan's family met Kriya family for the first time and they felt happy spending time with each other in a café

Kriya's Parents, Mr. & Mrs Arora liked Karan and his family.

On the same evening, Mr and Mrs Arora invited Mr. & Mrs Ahuja on dinner along with Rhea & Karan. They accepted the invitation.

When evening arrived, Karan called everybody as he was already waiting for everyone in the car.

 Mr Ahuja sat with Karan on the front & Mrs Ahuja sat behind with Rhea and he started driving towards Kriya's home. On the way, everybody was teasing Karan and he was blushing.

When they reached Kriya's home, Mr. & Mrs Arora greeted them on the door and took them to the living room where they sat and Kriya served them coffee & snacks.

 Suddenly, Mr Arora asked Karan to propose Kriya in front of them and Rhea also insisted the same to Karan, he looked in the eyes of his mother and father and got confident.

Karan called Kriya in the middle of the living room, bent on his knees and was having rose and ring in his hand and said,

"Hey beautiful
Since the time
You came in my life
My life took a beautiful turn
My heartfelt complete
Filled with love
For you and only you
I promise to take care
And respect you until
I'm alive and though
I'll never ever going to
Make you cry till my heart beats"

Will you marry me, my love?"

And he opened the box in which there was a beautiful platinum ring with her name.
Kriya felt shy and she blushed, "Yes I'll marry you."

Karan made her wear the ring on the ring finger and hugged her after that everybody applauded and celebrated their ring ceremony by having sweets and dinner together.

After dinner, Rhea hugged Kriya and congratulated her.

They got married on 11 August 2014 and both were living happily with Karan's family and Karan started spending time with his father and joined the family business.

Now, Kriya gave birth to her daughter whom they named "Krina". Rhea also got her graduation in humanities and now heading to New York for the job in a respectable company.

Sweta Mayur Vaidya

Mrs. Sweta Mayur Vaidya , is basically from Ahmedabad . Presently working as an Asst. Manager in Union Bank of India. She is a Post Graduate in English Literature from Gujarat University. She was born and brought up in Gandhinagar. Her Husband , Mr. Mayur Vaidya , is Director of Mayur's Academy of Dance (MAD). Mrs. Sweta Mayur Vaidya also plays an important part in his Husband's business.

Mrs. Sweta Mayur Vaidya is extremely passionate about dancing. She has done her Diploma in Performing Arts (Bharatnatyam) from Maharaja Sayajirao Gayakwad University (M . S. University , Baroda) . Acting is also one of her hobbies. She has done theatre in her early college days. Writing and reading is her hobby since she was a child. And thus, her inner wish to be a writer has developed. This is her first attempt as a contributing writer through " First Step Publishing".

Love at Every Sight

"So, is that it? " Jaanvi asked.

"Well, yes! " Rajveer added, "I thought you will cry, maybe you will be disheartened, but you seems to be so calm and having no complaints against what I said ".

"Will that make a difference to you? " Jaanvi asked she was almost on the verge of burst into tears.

"I don't have any answer".

"I know, that is why I am not questioning ". Jaanvi looked in the other direction. The sun was about to set and the sky was getting darker.

"Fine then, I think I should leave. "She added with a sigh.

"Are you sure? You don't want to say anything. Please say something ". Rajveer asked her with a heavy heart.

"I want to, I really want to. But I won't. Because I don't want to give you more pain. Because I know it takes hell lot of guts to say whatever you have just said. So it's better to keep quite. But I want to let you know one thing. "Tears rolled down her cheeks. She looked into his eyes, and added "Raj, you were and infect you are my life. I was mentally prepared for this." She held his face in her palms. "You are right at your place. So I don't want to blame you for anything. You would have married me if you could have. But if you can't. I am no one to force you to anything. I don't have any questions against your love because I know , what you are going through right now. It's just that, we are not fortunate enough to be together until the sunset of our lives. But it doesn't mean that we were not meant to be. "

Rajveer was silent; he was running out of words. He wanted to hold her tight and never wanted her to go. But he was helpless, he had to. He closed his eyes for a while, he saw a little girl with a handkerchief in her hand and sitting just next to him. She was not saying anything. But was crying uncontrollably, he couldn't see her crying but he had to. She stopped crying after a while, but she was still sobbing. She asked him, "Raj, what would I do now? Mumma left. Grand ma was saying she went to God's place and will never come back. But I miss her so much, why can't she just come back? "Rajveer was clueless. He didn't know what to say, all he could say was "you don't worry, Jaanvi, I am with you and will never leave you alone, trust me ". Very innocently that little girl asked him, "promise? ". He said, "Yes, promise ". And those words gave so much of relief to that girl. He opened his eyes, Jaanvi was still looking at him with tears in her eyes. She asked "what happened? " Rajveer was so upset with what all was going on. He said "Jaanvi, I m sorry, I could not keep my promise. "

"Ehh, stop it now. Stop feeling guilty. I am alright. And trust me, I will be all right always. And you better take care of yourself. I am getting late now. I think I should leave. "Jaanvi lied. She wanted to freeze this moment. Rajveer was her life. She was not getting late for anything. She wanted him to stop her. But she knew he won't. Rajveer dropped her at her place and while driving back to his home, he was actually on the drive of their past.

The sky was very cloudy. He thought it may rain today. He looked at the sky, he saw a face. A face of his life, Jaanvi. But the face was gloomy, her eyes were full of tears, she had so many questions in her eyes, but there was a smile on her lips, all the things on her face was contradictory. He stopped his car. Rested his head on the steering wheel and tears rolled down his cheeks. he started crying, he cried his heart out, he could not stop himself. His heart was aching. He kept on crying. Every moment he spent with her was running in his mind. He so badly wanted her right now. "I am sorry, Jaanvi, I am so so sorry. I don't want to let you go. How could I? I have seen my life, my future with you. Please forgive me, my love. Please forgive me." "He so badly wanted to go back to her. He wanted to rest his head in her laps. But he can't. His phone rang, that was his mother on the other side. He took the call, " beta, where are you , it's too late and it is raining heavily. When you are coming home?" He somehow managed to control his tears, "Maa, I am on the way." he disconnected.

He was sleepless. He took his phone and dialled her number. But disconnected within a second. He did not have guts to call her. On the other side, she was waiting, waiting so eagerly for his call, she had a little hope in her heart that he will call. Every night, they used to talk for hours. She used to tell him everything. About her work, office, what she have done, how badly she missed him in a particular situation. Rajveer used to listen to all her talks patiently. He loved the way she used to tell him everything. No matter how busy he was in his work he used to keep everything aside just to listen to all her chirpiness talks. Mobile phones were very new those days. For both of them, mobile was a blessing. Till then, they used to talk on landline phones but again, there was a limitation. This mobile phone was also a gift from Rajveer, as she could not afford such luxury thing.

Jaanvi was trying hard to sleep. But the thought process was not allowing her to sleep. She was 11 years old when she first met him. She used to go to tuitions after school and it was a Saturday. The school got over little early than weekdays and she was waiting for her tuitions to get the start. There was a small garden just next to their school where she was sitting on a swing to kill the time. Suddenly she heard some boys coming into that direction. He saw the boy from his school wearing school uniform and they were talking in a very loud voice. She could not understand what they were talking about. She looked at him and recognised that he was Rajveer, the most mischievous boy from her school. She became conscious and stood up from her swing. She took her school bag on her shoulder and started walking towards her bicycle. Rajveer did not pay attention to her as he was busy in chit-chatting with his friends. She left for her tuitions. That was the first time, she saw him.

After some one year, when they were now high school students, she saw a guy tracing her on a bicycle. That was Rajveer. She was afraid. She was little scared, he came to her and asked, " What is your name? "she said , " Jaanvi

". "Hmmm, do you stay nearby ? " , she said "umm, yes, but why you are asking this?" he said , "why you are getting scared? I am asking just like that. I am studying in the same school in which you are studying, if you don't mind can we go to school together from tomorrow? "

Jaanvi was surprised; she was little amused by the way he was asking her. She said, "okay! ".

And there they became friends. They started going school together, on the way to school, they used to share their likes-dislikes, their home works, and what not !. Both were just 13 years old. After school also, Rajveer used to teach Jaanvi how to play cricket. And in the account of repaying, Jaanvi started helping him with his homework. They became best friends; it was the year of 1999-2000. When school friends used to play games on the playground, they did not have many toys or modern equipment to play along. For them, hide and seek or badminton were the games. And Rajveer and Jaanvi loved to play together. Through their interactions, Rajveer came to know, that Jaanvi lost her father in very early age and she had no one else but her mother, who was working in some school as a primary teacher. They had limited income and Jaanvi used to study through her scholarships. She always borrowed school books from her senior's as she was not able to purchase books or stationery for her study. Many of the times, both used to share same textbooks for study. Jaanvi hardly had friends as she had Rajveer by her side. Rajveer was from a good and worthy family in which he had Maa, Papa, Brother and sister, and now, Jaanvi. They were so young to understand the meaning or the depth of love, but yes, since he met Jaanvi. He always used to adore her the most. For him, she was his everything, and everything means everything.

Suddenly, a big noise of thunderstorm happened. Jaanvi opened her eyes and looked around. It was still raining , she checked the watch , it was 3.30 am. She was sleeping with mobile in her hand. She checked but there was no missed call from Rajveer. She was so engrossed in her thoughts she couldn't understand when she fell asleep. She switched off the lights and tried to sleep again. She wanted to talk to Rajveer so badly.

Next day, she woke up so late. She started packing all her luggage and called for a cab. She left for a new city. She left all her memories behind. She left the love of her life , she switched off the mobile and left behind everything she had in that city, though she had not many things except Rajveer. She thought to call him once but she couldn't.

And she was in a new city, new people all around her. Everyone was unknown to her. Everybody was a stranger, she hired a cab and reached to her working women hostel. She had nothing as of now. She only had memories of Rajveer with him. From next day, she had to join her office. Everything was very new, the bed in the corner, a table to keep your daily used essentials. A mirror on the wall. She sat on the bed and looked around. It was all very old. There was another bed in the room and some clothes were already lying on it. The other girl must be at work, she thought. Rajveer couldn't sleep that night. He knew that she must have left for her new work today. He wanted to know whether she has reached or not? How her hostel is ? but he had no courage to call her. He wanted to call her. He wanted to talk to her. His mom came in the room, "Raj, are you not ready yet? We are getting late. Get ready fast, please". He nodded and went to the bathroom.

Today is the day when he was going to get marry to a girl whom he has never seen before.

He has always seen Jaanvi as her life partner. He has never ever imagined his life without her. She meant everything to him. From morning to late the evening to the late nights she was always there with him. He remembered the first time when he saw her in the garden, sitting all alone with thousands of thoughts in her mind. A little girl, sitting on a swing, looking here and there on a Saturday afternoon. It was something magical in that girl, something very unique which led him to the garden. But when that girl saw him she left the garden immediately. Since then, that girl was always on his mind. And when he again saw her after a year or so, he couldn't stop himself and immediately asked her if they can be friends. Till then, he was gathering guts to speak to her. He was finding reasons to be with her. And finally, he got the chance. Suddenly, there was a knock on the door. "Yes, come in , " he said. That was his younger brother. Rajveer was sitting on the chair. His brother came to him and sat on the bed. "what happened , *bhai* ? " he knew everything about their relationship. He knew that his elder brother must be in pain.

"Nothing, just like that". Rajveer replied.

"I know *Bhai*, you are so upset. But, all of us are helpless. Our society will never accept you getting married to the girl of another cast. You know really well how things are." His brother said.

"Yes, I understand. I know all the circumstances. And that is why I let her go. She was my life, she was my world. She meant everything to me. But she is gone now. Our society, our community strictly opposes inter-caste marriages. We are still living in the age where one has no right to decide one self's destiny. "Rajveer said with a sigh.

"But *bhai*, you always knew this."

"Yes, I always knew this. But I couldn't stop myself. I really want to be with her. I can't leave her alone. She has no one but me. She has nothing. And for me also, she is everything. She is my love. We have loved each other since long. Almost a ten years of relationship and I have loved her the most. I just can't imagine my life without her. I just want her here right now. I have only imagined her as my wife. I have seen my morning with her. I have seen my future with her. I can't believe she is gone. How would she survive without me? What she will do? She has never been alone. I have never let her be alone. She has not faced the world alone. She is in the unknown city, in between unknown people. She must be missing me, she must be looking for me. Where will she stay? Where will she go? What she will eat? Who will take care of her? What if she will fall ill?"

Someone knocked on the door.

126

"Son, let's go now. We are getting late", it was his dad
"Yes, Dad. Let's go."
And…. Rajveer got married.

SEVEN YEARS LATER :

It was a gloomy and cloudy evening..as if it is gonna rain
so hard.
Rajveer was driving through the main road and suddenly
saw a girl standing at the bus stop. He couldn't believe
his eyes. That was Jaanvi…

He stopped his car aside and wanted to assure whether
she is Jaanvi or not. And yes, she was Jaanvi.
The rush of thoughts came into his mind: "What is she
doing here ? Has she been transferred? Or she left the
job? "Hundred of thoughts came across in his minds.
"Should I go and talk to her ?" Rajveer asked himself.

"oh! I think it's going to rain so hard, I should take a cab.
" Jaanvi was thinking to hire a cab and a car came just
next to her.
She was stunned, she was frozen.
"Raj? Umm.. Ahhh.. "She was still in a beautiful shock.
She didn't know what to say, what to do, how to react.
she was just blank !! Totally blank !! Rajveer's eyes were
full of tears.
The only words that came out from his mouth were
"Jaan!"

It started raining suddenly and the real rain was from Rajveer and Jaanvi's eyes. Both set down in a car and started talking. "So? " Rajveer started the conversation: "so, you shifted here?" "Um, well, yes. " Jaanvi replied. Still amazed with what all was going on. "Got married ? Rajveer asked. "eh? No! Not yet " Jaanvi replied, paused for a while. "where is your Family ?" Jaanvi asked . "Right behind you." Rajveer pointed to the back seat of the car. Jaanvi turned back and saw a little girl, sleeping like an angel, very innocent , very charming and very beautiful. "Oh ! that's your daughter ?"

"Yes " Rajveer replied. "she is so cute and adorable." Jaanvi paused , and asked, "where is your wife then?" "We are separated." "Wait, what?" Jaanvi was taken aback." What are you saying?" "Yes, she left me and my daughter," Rajveer said. "What? Why? "She couldn't believe what she has just heard. Who can leave such a cute doll alone? She was thinking in her mind. "Yes, you heard it right. She had her own reasons." The little girl opened her eyes and was little conscious when she saw a lady sitting in their car. "Papa..!!" the little girl was little sleepy yet. "Jaanvi, say hi to Jaanvi Aunty!!".

For a second, for a moment, Jaanvi couldn't believe what she just heard. Rajveer named her daughter after her, that was something very soothing. Jaanvi asked that little girl if she wants to come to her. Little Jaanvi immediately agreed and came in the lap of Jaanvi. Jaanvi felt like she wants nothing more than this moment, she has never asked more from life. She looked at little Jaanvi and felt as if she was falling in love with that little girl. She looked at Rajveer.

He didn't have words but yet he wanted to say something. He said: "Jaanvi was my world and today Jaanvi is my world. But now, today also, I can't ask you for anything. I left you when you needed me the most. I broke all my promises, I left you alone. I am your culprit. Jaanvi, you don't know how much I have missed you. There was not even a single moment in all these years when you were not there in my mind, my thoughts. You were everywhere. But.. but… "

Jaanvi put his hand on Rajveer's mouth. " shhh… Rajveer you now very well, you don't need to say anything. I can still understand your silence . You don't need to put your feelings into words. You know what, I feel in love with a guy at the age when I didn't even know what love is. Though it was not loved at the first time. Because as long as we grew together I was falling in love with you more and more with every upcoming day. And today, I feel in love with myself. I feel in love with Jaanvi. It is not like, there is something like sympathy or any kind of favour for you or this little girl. But I still can feel the love in everything you love. You named your daughter, Jaanvi. Because you wanted me to be around you, knowingly or unknowingly, I was always there. And you can't deny it."

Jaanvi stopped for a pause and then again said: "You had your own reasons and your limitations seven years back, but today, I won't let you go. Not because I love you but because you have loved me more than anything. Love never need proofs, it has no excuses. Love itself is very beautiful and today, I want to be with you not because our age old relationship but for this little Jaanvi. Who made me realise that love happens just once and the rest is just life. Rajveer, marry me. More than your wife, I want to be Jaanvi's mother, I want to raise her. " Rajveer was speechless. And very happy from inside. Because he had both the Jaanvi's of his life by his side.

Shivani Pathak

Shivani Pathak, residing at surat, has completed her Post graduation in M.Sc (I.T) from Gujarat University and is currently working with Ratnakala Software. She is fond of writing and believes in penning her emotions. She believes in experimenting new and creative things. She shows her deep interest in music and philosophy. She believes in living life every moment, expressing her inner soul and making others happy.

Two Hearts That Beat As One

I have heard that "life is a surprise!!!" but it could turn out to be such surprising and was really a big surprise in itself. The story revolves around life of local people like u and me. It's not a huge story it may resemble a part of our life or you may relate yourself to some of it.

There was a girl who recently passed her 12th examination and was waiting for her results. A studious girl after all!!. She was never interested in anyone's life, a jolly person who had her own world in herself. She had a couple of friends not much close though because these days she was busy with her studies and as such interfering was never her nature. But she was being loved by all for her kindness and loyalty. So, as she was waiting for her results she had a long vacation after the stress-full board year so she had enough time for herself and was getting into the world slowly. This beautiful girl was called "Amruta". She was from a maharashtrian family.

She was active on social media these days and apparently had made many good friends. One fine day she received a message from a person she hardly knew. That was not a big deal, as it was a general message. They had a good conversation and suddenly the person asked her: "did you tagged me in a video?" she was surprised by the question itself. A bit worriedly Amruta asked :"a video?" I never tagged anyone yet!! Well the conversation started in this way and who knew it would give such a wonderful turn to their life.

They apparently knew each other as the boy was working as part-time assistant in the high school classes where she was studying. But they didn't knew each other personally as he has left the job when she joined the classes. Only 1month was left and they hardly had faced each other so this conversation was as good as a stranger's conversation for them. They had to introduce right from their names to each other.

Amruta : "Hii myself Amruta. How are you?"

Ashutosh : "I am fine!! So what are you doing now?? How much did u score in 12th?"

Amruta : "I got distinction! I score 80.88 percentile."

Ashutosh : "wow that's a great score!! Congo"

And so like this the chat continued. After few days they came to know it was a spam and due to that a video was being sent to everyone on behalf of her name. She was not in fault. Days passed and they talked for hours together. They started knowing each other. Their thoughts were quite similar and their nature too. Once he asked for her phone no. and then apart from social media he used to send her jokes on phone. But she never replied to them. After few days passed like this Ashutosh finally called her. That was the first time they heard each other's voice. He had called her just to talk normally but she was very surprised as how can anyone call straight away like this? He then somehow asked her, "why are you not replying to my text messages?"

"She was quiet for sometimes and then said, "I would reply from now onwards."

But the thing was Amruta had never texted anyone yet, as she had her first phone in 11th std. so she was hesitating in messaging anyone directly. Those days he was in Pune. He was a typical Gujarati boy, from a middle class family. He had a very nice small family. From his childhood itself he was very fond of his mother and she had brought him up with great efforts. He went there as he was offered a job in Pune.

Then the days passed they grew more close to each other. They used to share every single thing that happened in their life. Ashutosh didn't had a great childhood. He was a bit sad and lonely in his life. At a very young age he had started working for the family. He had many responsibilities on his shoulder. In a nutshell he had never lived his life as a child happily or spending the time like other boys do. He had to be mature at young age and it was the reason that he was very introvert kind of person. He never had many friends. But he was a friend of himself. He used to write diary in which he had described his wait for his soulmate which he was eagerly waiting for. He had described the nature, her looks, her personality and each detail he wanted to have in his better half. A year ago, when he was feeling too alone everyday he used to write this diary. This diary was very close to his heart. He had never shown it to anyone. It was his piece of heart which he wanted to share only with his life partner.

He had no one to share his life with. He always wrote his feelings in diary and never expressed them to the outside world. But talking to Amruta made him feel much better as he could share things with her, trust her. By now they had talked a lot and had understood each other's nature really well. All those small things which matter, and which no one else knew about him were all well understood by Amruta. They became the best friends. Now this was the time when both of them had thought that no one else than the other person would be better for them as best friend. The friendship was like never seen before, it was a forever kind of friendship in all means.

Suddenly one fine day Amruta found a message in her inbox telling..

"I am sorry but I don't want to have contact with any girl . I have deleted all the girls from my account so I m even deleting you .Please don't try to contact me or message me by any means"

Reading this, she was deeply shocked. She never understood what happened and why he did so. She tried to contact him but he had already removed her from his social account. She was wondering what was her mistake? Did she say anything which she should have not said? Or anything else, many questions crept into her mind and after a long time she had got someone as best friend in her life and suddenly this was what happened. She couldn't take it she burst out into tears. Many different thoughts came to her mind. She had shared her life with that stranger. At her home her mother used to ask what happened why now he never calls you. At first every now and then he used to talk. Is that all ok?

She had no answer to all these questions. Nor she had answers to the questions in her mind. But things have changed for her, by now he had been very close to her as a friend. They shared every moment. So she was getting mad each time she recalled the past time. Every day she used to go to his social media profile just to check his

135

activity whether he is fine or not! Just to get a clue as for why he suddenly took such a big step.

On the other side the boy was also in the same situation. He too was not happy with his life. He was even frustrated with the entire work load he had in his office. He was even frustrated with his personal life ups and down. He was not able to adjust himself to things around him. He used to stay in frustration and anger all the time. He too was feeling the same what the girl went through. But then why did he do that? He was really feeling guilty for leaving her alone after such friendship.

Time passed, everyone says time heals all things and as time pass we forget people. But this was not true in this case. As time passed the girl had strong hopes, one day she will get her best friend back, as her friendship was true and from heart. She strongly believed he will come back. And this is what happened!!! After the long period of 3 months, one fine day the girl received a friend request again... with a message: "sorry for what I did, I would like to be your friend if u can forgive me".

Seeing this, she was on cloud nine. She could not believe her eyes. Nothing mattered for her what he did, how he left her the only thing she was concerned was she got her best friend back. She immediately accepted his friend request and forgives him. With time they started their normal talks again but she was constantly asking him the reason for what he did. He ignored few times but then one afternoon he said: "I have cultivated different feelings for you. You mean more than a friend to me, I like spending time talking with you and I have stared liking you. I don't know what is it but I am enjoying this new feelings for you. Please don't take it in a wrong way. Don't you feel happy talking to me?? Don't you feel the same things?? "

After some time he again said "it was this reason that I went away from your life. I started feeling whether if I like this girl, What will the society think? How will we look together?" The boy was tall and handsome; the girl was short and beautiful. "Are these feeling correct to express to you? Will society accept our friendship??? What people will think?" All these questions drew me away thinking if I will not stay in your life all these things won't affect me. But this never happened. And I can't lose our friendship because of all these feelings. I thought about this and I felt that to have such feelings is not a wrong thing. "This was my reason. If you think I did nothing wrong and we should have our friendship intact then I am always there but if you think it is wrong then I will agree with whatever you say." Said Ashutosh

Now it was all up to her whether to keep the friendship or to leave. She was quiet for a long time. Then she replied: "even I had such feeling in those days when we were not talking. I was completely lost and I found I couldn't stay away though we don't feel anything in that way still we can be best of friends no matter what".

Her reply made him feel so comfortable that he no more has to hide anything from her. This was the starting stage of their love story; they had already fallen for each other unknowingly. Now it was the day when he was returning back home after a long time. He came home for 7 days and in that they decided to meet each other. This was their first meeting after all. He texted, "see you at lunch in Sankalp restaurant I'll be there by 12".

On 30th may 2010, both of them reached the restaurant at the same time. She had covered her face, they both parked the vehicles next to each other and when she removed her scarf he finally had a glance of her. They both didn't understand what to talk, how to start, what to say!!! Finally they were comfortable. They went into the restaurant. As it was afternoon the restaurant had no one, it made them more uncomfortable. The atmosphere seemed to be made as if on date!! Only two of them with the most romantic music played "ek ladki ko dekha to esa laga..." Somehow they came through all this and it was friendship day for them. They exchanged friendship belts, and finally waved a good bye. This is how unknowingly even the universe wanted them to make fall in love with other, things turned up to give them quality time alone always. After few days he went back to his work.

On June 13th 2010, around 12:28 am at night having a normal chat with him suddenly she saw those three wonderful letters of her life.. " I LOVE U <3 "with a heart. Seeing that she was so shocked and surprised, she couldn't speak nor type, tears rolled down her eyes with a wonderful smile on lips. She didn't understood what to say and what to do; she had all type of thoughts in her mind in those few seconds. The world seemed changed for her. But with a heart filled with love and no other thought of, the rest of the world she said: "I LOVE U TOO <3".

After that their life was filled with never ending love, care, happiness all seemed to be perfect. They both were very happy. They could not meet often, they could meet only once in 6 months. And this was the biggest problem "the time" even after being in a relation they had no time for each other to spend together. But their love was very strong even if they could not meet for months together. They shared a wonderful bond of trust and loyalty. They had firmly decided to share their life with each other no matter what. Distance never came in their way. Even the proposal was on social media, they were not face to face but the love in their heart was deeply connected. So six months went and he again arrived home. This time he even came to attend his cousin's marriage. He was very close to his mother; he used to share everything with his mother. His mother was his role model. When he came home, Amruta invited him at her house. On the next day itself he came to meet her. They meet outside without telling anyone that was the time they shared their feelings to each other. Then both of them came home, her mother too was very happy to meet him. She recalled, she had already met him before in the high school class meeting which he conducted. She said, I still remember "tall smart, handsome guy in suit perfectly dressed and addressing all the parents sitting there. Greeted everyone with smile and conducted the meeting for an hour" she said I still remember u told us: "your daughter is not good in chemistry she needs to improve herself"

He was so shocked listening all this. He agreed about the meeting but he didn't remember about meeting her mother before. But then their bond grew so much that her mother used to consider him her own son. He used to visit her home whenever he came to his hometown. The relation was far deep than a true mother and son relation. Meanwhile when he came to her house , the next day his mother asked him :"is she only your good friend or more than that???" he was very close to his mother and never wanted to lie or hide things from her so he said :"for now she is my best friends and I do have feelings for her but still we are not at a stage to tell you whether I ll marry her or not , but ya I am very happy with her" his mother was very flexible and never forced him to marry the girl she likes or marry the girl of their community. So she said if you are happy with her and if you feel u will be able to live your life with her then I have no issues. You are free to love the girl of your choice. So for now his mother was on their side. Gradually with the passing time, her mother also asked her the same question. To which she also told the truth. Her mother was a bit worried she was tensed if her father comes to know about this then? Who will be responsible? How can you just do that? But in her mind she knew the boy was apt for her. She tried to convince her not to love him, she would get anyone else. But the girl was firm with her decision and seeing this, her mother also added her support. Now the days were happy they never had to lie anyone about their relation and moreover they had got the permission from their parents so they had no fear. Only thing was the girl's dad. It was very hard to make him agree for this relation. The problem which might come with this relation was they were from different families. The boy was from a Guajarati family and the girl was from a Maharashtrian family. They both had different cultures. Moreover her father didn't like him. He always went away from home when he used to come. He disliked him without any reason.

On the other hand with the passing time and growing togetherness the boy felt he should share his diary with her. She is the only one with whom he can share things. So one day he just sent her the diary and asked her to read out his life and asked whether she would hold his hand in this life. He had many problems at home. He had a very small house with one room and kitchen. At a very young age he started working for the family. He had some clashes with his father. He never talked to him. So it was all his mother, his world was limited to her. When he came to pune his job salary was 12000/- . He had very hard times staying away from his family making his living here as well as managing his family in his hometown. He was in search for a better job but every time he tried he failed. The diary read many things about the type of girl he wanted in his life. And before the girl came in his life he was already in love with the imaginary idol he had created in his diary. He had showed immense love for her in a variety of ways. He had showed all his inside part of a person in single diary. She was so heart felt to read that. After having completed the reading she texted him is it that u have described me??? He said this is what I wanted to make u realize too. The imaginary person whom I used to visualize from years before is exactly what you are. And I have shared this with you because now I feel, I am ready to accept you as a life partner. This is what I am. She was quite, then she said I ll hold your hand in all the situations of our life. I don't care what things are and how situations will fall for us, but I promise to stay my entire life with you. The diary proved to be the stepping stone of their life. From now they actually loved each other the way they were. They wanted to stay by their side for the rest of their life. Their love grew more stronger, they could even feel each other through words. There was a great power in their love.

This time when he came back to his hometown, they met each other and it was something special than a normal meet. They spent a whole day together. Amruta bunked her college and they went for a movie, had a ride and enjoyed the wonderful feeling of being together. It was the first time he hugged her. She could feel the entire world in his arms. The feeling they had of first hug, knowing someone so closely for the first time , the magic of falling in love was immensely strong and beautiful.

This time when he came it was his birthday!!! She wanted to give him a surprise but only her mother knew about their relation, moreover she had to hide all this from her father. So she planned something. That day she called him home around 1pm to have lunch with them. When he came home he was totally surprised. His eyes could not believe, there in the main hall a beautifully decorated table was placed with a wonderful fruit cake , a shampain, a heart-touching card and ofcourse a lot of roses. All of the three, lit the candle and enjoyed his birthday. They spent the afternoon together, had lunch and made a memory for life. Days passed happily and the routine continued. He was again busy with his work.

After few months, he started being frustrated; he was worried because of his job. There were many responsibilities he had. He finally went for an interview that was held in Bombay. Everything went fine but again he was rejected. He was feed up with rejection. But with her support he became strong to face again. She never left him alone in any condition. And finally he got job offer. It was from Aurangabad. He was selected there. Now the question was he had to shift to Aurangabad. There was no problem for language as such, because he had already learnt to speak Marathi. Now for him a new place, a new job, new people and new work load. Before shifting to Aurangabad he came to his hometown. They both met each other. He very lovingly and caringly explained her:" Amruta, now I am shifting my job, I may be busy there, I won't be able to give you appropriate time so please take care and do not get worried". She also consoled him:"everything will be fine and you will definitely shine one day". With a heavy heart they parted away.

He went to Aurangabad. He was very busy with his work, moreover he had to rent a house for himself, manage all his living on his own. So days were very tough and he could not even message her or talk to her. Even this was making him a bit angry that he could not even give time to his loved ones. He was struggling a very tough time. On the other hand she was also worried for him as they could not talk for a long time. She many times tried to talk but they could hardly talk which was not enough for her. She wanted to make sure he was comfortable there, her worry and care was perfect on her side. But his frustration of job and settlement was also right on his side. They both made their best efforts to understand each other. But at some point of time they failed. They started having small fights. They started fighting on small things which actually had no value to be given, but the time raised the issues. Small fights took large turns. His frustration and anger blew out on her. One day it went too far and both of them spoke such words to each other which they should have not said. He said:"I don't want this relation any more as I cannot keep you happy and give you enough time. I have had enough and now want peace of mind and live alone". Listening all this she also replied:"fine if you don't want nor do I want" but this was all in anger and somewhere ego. She was broken into pieces. She could not control her tears and without thinking she just burst out. Her mother saw this side of her for the first time. She had never cried in front of anyone before. Her mother was deeply sad seeing her daughter's condition. She had to somehow hide all this from her father and other family members.

2 days passed she didn't had food and finally one day she wrote a suicide note to him and went away from home as usual for college. When he read that email he was shocked he tried to call her, but she didn't answered his calls. He tried to call her friends and finally he called her mother. He told everything. She returned late than usual time at home. Her mother was too worried but when she came, she never showed her. After sometime her mother said I know all things and scolded her for being so stupid. She told her you have to choose between me and him. You make your decision firm. She had no other option left than leaving her relation at such point.

On the other hand he too was not happy with the decision he took in anger. He also cried a lot being a man. But the time had gone and this is what it was meant to be. In the starting days of separation they had a lot of hatred for each other. They never wanted to see each other's face. They had started believing there is nothing called love. All are selfish and mean in this world. They had made their mind of not even being in contact of each other. But as time passed and when both of them calmed down, things took a clear vision. They both were equally suffering and missing each other. They couldn't contact each other even if they wished to. Somewhere they really still loved each other, even after being separated they were not separate, their hearts were still beating for each other. But they didn't wanted to accept this truth out of ego. So they tried to live each day with a smile and tears in their eyes pretending they can live without each other. Days and months passed. They had no idea what the other person's condition was. They even never kept their trust on other person when they themselves set this example. So again their lonely life overpowered. Amruta somehow had her friend to share things. But Ashutosh was all alone and broken down. He neither could nor show his condition to the world nor he could share with anyone and could not even run away from situations. He faced them all alone.

Finally the day came when he had to return to his hometown. He was arriving by plane. She somehow took the information from their mutual friend. He had a habit of forgetting things very often. So with the help of their mutual friend she conveyed all the messages to him to properly take the list of things he needed. Once for a while he even said to their friend:"I don't know why but the way you are listing things I feel Amruta is telling all this, it is exactly what she would have done". He never knew it was her who was doing it.

He arrived home. She was so restless, she wanted to meet him. After all she knew she can't hate him in her life. Whatever had happened was not a concern to her. She just wanted to make sure he was fine. Her restlessness grew more and more. She talked to her mother. She said I will not tell you anything you do what you want. Sitting in her room alone, failing to control her feelings for him, forgetting the ego she just dialed his number. The bell rang but no one answered, after sometime time the call was received. None of them spoke a single word. Their silence was enough to convey their feelings. After few minutes he said:"hello" tears came down her eyes listening his voice after a long time. Controlling herself and not letting him know, she continued:"hello, how are you". He recognized her voice and stood still. Said:"m fine and u?" she said:"just called you like that, ok then bye". He too waved bye and the call ended. All those wonderful memories flashed in her mind. She was into them and suddenly again the phone rang. Yes!!! It was his call, she picked up and on the other side, and he burst into tears. He couldn't control himself; with a heavy heart he said I want to meet you. She tried to control and console him made him feel better and explained him. But he was forcing to meet once. She agreed to meet him the next day.

They meet in a coffee shop. There after seeing each other, again feel in love. They expressed their feeling when they were apart. They both confessed, they can't live without each other. They both need each other. Unitedly both said whatever may happen we will not get separated now. We are meant to live with each other not without each other. So finally they decided to continue their relation with the same feeling. The next day Ashutosh organized a date for her in a 5 star hotel. They both went and coincidently they both dressed perfectly matching to each other. There in the hotel, to her surprise he had a gift for her. He gave a medium sized box beautifully wrapped in red paper with a heart on top. She opened the gift with a beautiful smile on her face. To her surprise there was a rose. Not a simple, ordinary rose but a gold rose. Yes he gave a gold rose which would always stay fresh like their never ending love. Seeing such a costly gift Amruta refused to take it home. As soon as she refused his eyes were filled with tears saying:" we can't even meet, nor can I gift u anything fearing your parents, nor can we go out, nor can we openly talk, I can't even express how much I love you. I don't want such life. I want to be by your side. I want to take you with full right please atleast accept this gift." He forced her and she had no option but to accept it.

Days passed and their love grew stronger and stronger with time. No silly fights nor the distance affected their love. He even got promotions finally and he proved himself. He was known in his company for his hard work. He was now a Dept .Manager. Things changed ,life changed. By now his entire family knew about Amruta.

With the flick of eyes 5 years flew away with still their bond the same as on 1st day. Now he was a Manager of the company. All things were settled. He had built his home, brought up his family and was a very responsible man now. On the other side Amruta had also completed her studies with distinction and was awarded by the university. She also got placed in a software company from the college itself. Everything was on track so by now a long time had passed and they decided to tell about their relation to her parents.

So one fine day Ashutosh came home. He came home at 6:30 sharp . He told her father that he wants to talk with him. But as always her father out of anger left home. He came after 2 hours but Ashutosh was still waiting for him. Finally he gathered all his courage and asked him:" sir, I would like to marry your daughter, if you permit. We both like each other and would like to spend our life together." Her father was very rude to him. He never replied properly to him rather disrespected him. Still he was very patient and polite. He told , taking her father's hand in his hand :" I can very well understand your condition sir , she is your daughter and you should take your time to accept me. You can even inspect things you like about me. I am ready to wait till you answer."

He then quietly went away. Her Dad reacted for few days and showed his anger in many ways. But as time passed all things felt in place. Many times things went out of box when this matter was discussed.

We all will have to wait to know what happens in their life. Will they marry each other? Will their love will win everyone's heart. What happens in their life. But one

148

thing is sure they got the love of their life again in the same person. And this time it was true and never ending love which no one can deny. And they have also understood the power of love which in future life they will never again underestimate.

Ravina Kaniyawala - Riya

Ravina Kaniyawala, Born on 12th November 1993 in Surat, Gujarat - a Surti girl. She has completed her master degree in M.Sc(IT) and doing internship from an IT firm. She is a software developer(iOS Developer). The people around her knows her by Riya. She is graduated from J.P.Dawar Institute of Information Science and Technology and is currently working in Ratnakala Software Pvt. Ltd.

Riya is a passionate writer and a motivating person. She is addicted to writing what life teaches her in every step. Her world rolls around her family. She loves to look at life with the positive attitude. She believes in a strong and pure love. She wants to travel the world and travelling gives her passion for writing and thinking. Love is her strength which supports her in her good and bad and always motivates her. New places give her the immense of peace and improves her thoughts and help her in writing.

She loves drawing and painting. Colours gives her new vision to look forward toward life. She builds herself to face every challenge that comes across her. She finds love the very pure thing on the earth. Nature is the best surrounding which gives her positivity and peace. She wants to open the school for physical handicap people one day. She is young floating, jolly kind of person. Who want to achieve the goals and success in her life with hard work and support.

She has written short stories in 6 anthologies and Falling for Love Again is the second one with First Step Publishing. Riya is going to come up with her novel soon. She finds her readers as a great support in her endeavour of books.

To know more about her you can contact her at @riya.kaniyawala – Facebook. Or you can mail her at rkaniyawala123@gmail.com.

Riya Kaniyawala is her pen name.

Stranger became my Soul-mate.

I am married to the one who is just the stranger to me. I love the one who used me and left me, and I got married to the one who knows everything about me yet wants me. Does he too want a physical relation with me? Is he also thirsty of sex? I am sitting in unfortunately now OUR bedroom and it is our 1st night. I wonder what my life has lead to, where I used to dream my life with Manan and now I am here with Abhay just the stranger. I was lost in past.

(It was my birthday and Manan and I decided to meet.)
I dressed well and asked mom (Who really is my step mom) to go out.
"What type of girl are you? The girl wants to celebrate her birthday whose mother died because of her on just next day of her birthday. Just shame on you Deepali. Do whatever you want I am not your mom and you don't need my permission." my step mom said the things which left me with a teary eye.
Sana (My stepsister but more like my real sister) just stops her in between, Mom, Watch your words. What was her mistake in aunt's death? And at least spare her. Today it's her birthday.
I had no mood to meet Manan but Sana just dragged me and I meet him.
Manan hugged me but he didn't once ask me why my eyes were looking this dull? Can't he find that after one year of relationship or he don't want to spoil the mood so

he didn't ask? Sana told me she will be returning in one hour and left us alone.

He brought a cake for me and bought a dressed for me and he wanted me to wear it for him.

When I came wearing that dress. He came close to me and hugged me. He came closer and tries to kiss but I pushed him back. He got bit angry on me but it was my birthday so he did not utter a word.

I return to home. I was happy that I spent at least a good day.

Manan: "Deepali, I want to say something.'Let's get married'. I am serious. You want commitment and I am ready to give it to you." asked Manan.

"I don't know how to react on this. What are you saying? Mom will never accept this." - I replied.

Manan - "One day we have to tell, then why not today? I have told everything to my parents and they are ready to accept us. You talk to your parent and rest of thing I will look after."

I don't know how I tell this to mom dad so I told Sana about this.

The next day we decide to convey the truth about my relationship first to dad and then to mom and Sana decide to accompany me.

We entered into his room.... Dad, I want to share something with you. I don't know how you are going to react but I want to say...

Dad holds my hand and reply to me - "Sit. What you want to share?"

Me: "Dad, I love someone and I want to get married to that guy. I don't know how you will react. But I do love him a lot."

Mom heard everything and she just came and slaps me so hard. And she yelled at dad.

"I told you always that cut the wings of her. I know she could do something like this only. What could we expect from a girl who killed her own mother? "

Mom, Stop all this, I don't kill her. And I get another slap by my dad.

This time, I can't control my tears. He slapped me because for the first time. I reverted back to her. Where was he until these days when she was continuously abusing me? I really can't call anyone as my people, who really cares and loved me except Sana and Manan. And these guys don't want me to marry even Manan? Mom took my phone and warned me not to meet Manan ever again. And she told dad to find some boy for me and get me married soon.

"Sana, I want to meet Manan once can you call him and fixed my meeting?" - I ask for a favour.

She called him and told everything. She booked a room for us in a hotel and we decided to meet there. The next day Sana somehow manages to take me out and dropped me to the hotel.

Manan planned everything to cheer my mood. As I entered the room I was surprised by seeing flowers all around. He just dragged me inside and hugged me. He bought a wine and He poured two glasses and offered me one.

"Manan, you know I don't drink. I will be in no sense if I drink this." - I replied by rejecting his offer for the drink.

"Just, trust me, baby. I am here and I will do nothing. Have faith and drink and you will forget all your pain. "- he consoles me.

I took it and we started to drink. We spoke a lot. I cried a lot. I told him how mom and dad slapped me and warned me not to meet him. Now how could we get married? I am scared what if they don't get convinced?

Manan:" Shh. . . keep quite. Don't think much; saying which he just came close to me and kissed me on my lips. I pushed him back once but he again came close and kissed me, this time, I don't know whether it was wine or my pain but I kissed him back."

He came very close to me opened up my hair; held me so tight. He dragged me to the bed and loved me. I loved him back. I didn't want this frankly before marriage but I couldn't stop him. I was in no sense while I was doing so. Once we made love he just got up and got ready, he didn't speak to me even once. I was furious. My head was spinning. I could not understand what was happening to me.

He came closer to me and said "GOODBYE, Baby." I don't know why he said so. He just left the room. I didn't understand what was happening to me, whether it was a dream or not? I somehow managed to dress up. The next moment I know is, I find myself on the bed and my room which was locked from outside.

I got up and I seriously couldn't remember what had happened to me. I knocked the door very hard but no one came to open it. I cried very hard. I wanted to ask

Sana what had happened. Why am I trapped in my own house like this? I want to talk to Manan why he just left the room like that. I wanted many of the answers. I hit the door many of the time but no one opened it.

In the night, when everyone got asleep Sana opened the door and came to the room. She just hugged me and told everything will be alright soon.

What happened Sana? Why am I locked like this? Why Manan just left me like that? I was in the hotel how I reach here? I asked.

Sana: Manan called and told me to take you home. When I opened the door you were on the floor. You were heavily drunk. I tried waking you up but you did not. I called Manan many of times but he didn't receive the call. Then I found the packet of used condom on the floor. And despite all this Manan called to our landline and that jerk told everything to mom that you came to meet her and you had sex. And he told that he got what he wanted and told mom to handle you.

You know mom, right? She called me and told me to bring you home immediately. When we reached home they asked you and you too admitted that you had sex with him and she locked you in the room. And Deepali, you know what? They had fixed the meeting with one guy and he is going to come to see you tomorrow.

Deepali, Manan just used you. He doesn't love you at all. He even doesn't want to talk to you once. I know this all is so difficult for you to digest but you have to do, you are very strong.

And she just left the room. The night was just sleepless for me. I could not carry that the guy I loved for one year just used me like a paper and thrown me. All this he was doing just to have me? Why being physical is just the priority of a boy?

****

The next day mom opens my room and told me that Abhay, is going to meet me as they saw my picture and his parents are interested in me. And Abhay too liked me.

I dressed but I have no interest to meet who so ever he is. I welcome them, They asked me few question and they insisted us to chat alone for some time. Sana takes us to the terrace and leaves us to talk.

"I know this is so awkward for both of us. So let me cut the silence. I am Abhay. I have my own business and I am staying in Pune and my parents are here in Bombay. I am staying alone there and now I need someone to support me. " - Abhay broke the silence

"See, I want to be very frank with you that I have no interest in you. I am meeting you because my parents want me to have arranged marriage. I love someone and I just had a breakup with him yesterday due to some reason and I am in no sense that I could marry you. And yes, one another thing is I am a murderer I had killed my mother so you decide whether you want to marry me or not? The choice is up to you as no one is going to ask me my choice whatever you decide will be considered final". - I replied very rudely.

He, just give me the smile. I don't know what that smile is for. Does he don't bother that I had affair with someone? Does he just same like Manan who too needs to use me like a paper?

I was sure that he will say no. My mom, dad was waiting for their phone call to know their answer. And to my surprise, Abhay is ready to marry me.

My parents decide to have a simple marriage function. I am not ready for this marriage. I don't want to marry to the stranger. I wonder if one can use me after knowing him for more than one year then what this person will do to me who is completely stranger to me. How is this man going to treat me? I think he knows my secret and I am again going to have slave life. Here mom is taunting and after marriage, he will do the same.

I try very hard to convince everyone that I don't want to have marriage but no one did understand except Sana. Sana can't do anything now. I don't want it at all. I don't want that stranger.

I miss my own mom a lot. I wish if she could be here nothing like this could have happened to me ever. I don't want to have arranged marriage as I don't trust a stranger and I don't believe them.

Do I try to find a reason why Abhay is ready to accept me? What was the reason behind that? But I find nothing. I hugged Sana and cried that day a lot. From tomorrow even Sana will be not there to support me and I am going to all alone to deal with Abhay.

I was all dressed up and all were waiting for Abhay to come to the *mandap*. I was scared with marriage but I have no option left. Though I am married to him but I don't accept him with my heart.

And finally, I got married to him. Now I am Mrs Abhay. I was so upset, I couldn't even digest that Manan just left me and I was tied to Abhay for the rest of my life.

I was lost in my thoughts. And suddenly door open, And I was back in the reality. I find Abhay in the room. I don't know how to tell him that I don't want to have sex. How do I tell him that he is just the stranger and how could I trust him for the rest of my life? I scared what if he gets angry if I tell him I don't want to get physical at this stage. I am so scared that I stare at the floor and did not face him. I recall the time when Manan got so angry if I decline to have sex. I scared how this man gonna treat me if I will ignore him?.

Abhay entered the room he got fresh and come to the bed and said:

"Listen Deepali, I know this all is strange for you as you don't want to have this marriage. You have many of questions in your mind that why I chose you. I know I am a puzzled guy for you right now. But I assure you that you will get all the answers very soon. And don't worry I will never force you to love me back. Even I don't want to have our 1st night now."

I just cut him from between and reply,

"If you think by doing this you will impress me then you are wrong Abhay. I am not interested in this marriage though you force me to get married to you and I can't forgive you for that. And assuring that you don't want sex I can't digest that. "

He smiled and said, don't think much you will get all your answer soon. I am not like your Ex. Don't worry I am sleeping on the couch. You sleep here and once we reach Pune, I will sleep in another room so you don't feel awkward. But here let not anybody know about this. Good night.

I don't know I find something different in him, what was that but I like his honesty at least.

Abhay has his own business and we need to reach Pune so we left his parents home. He shows me his house. It was just beautiful. He saw me his room and asked me if I want to stay there he will shift to next room. But I decline and reply that I will shift to another room.

He left the house and I was all alone. I was so alone and I know I have to fight against my own thoughts again. The memories of Manan, the complaints about Manan will get back to me. The memories of Manan just make my week. Does all Manan want till the one year was sex only? I had many of the questions against him, and I don't know whether I will get their answers ever or not? What was my fault? Why no one loves me? My own mom left me and my dad got married to another woman. Does ever I tell him that he choose someone else beyond my mom then why they keep blaming me for my mom's death?

I know each fact very well till this year though I never mentioned to them. My dad desperately wants the child and doctor told them she is not ready to conceive the child. She is not that fit then only everyone demands a child and she decides to give a birth to me. And after she gave born to me, the very next day she died. Why no one blames family for forcing her to have a child? I was not even known to this. No one asks me how I felt when I get to know that my mom died because of me. I was not responsible for that but until this year my stepmom used to taunt me every now and then to blame me for killing my mom. Why did no one ask me how I felt when I got to know my mom died to give birth forcefully? I was so busy with my thoughts and I don't know what the time was and I find Abhay is just back from office.

"I am so sorry, I had not cooked anything. I was so lost in my thoughts that I don't know what time it is. It will not happen from next time. I remember when my dad return from home and food is not ready how he scold mom and I am afraid what Abhay is going to do." - I said coming out of my thoughts.

Abhay replies softly, "That's okay Deepali, No need to be this formal. We will go out and have dinner. Will you join me or should I get a parcel for you?"

(This man really shocked me. I was mesmerised with his answer.)

I will join you. Could you just give me 10 min to change? - I asked.

Yaa, sure take your time. I need to get fresh too. And yes, be comfortable to dress whatever you are comfortable with. I don't have any problem with that.

I wonder, does he really like this? Or he did to impress me? I get ready and I was waiting for him. He asked me what I want to eat and I reply whatever you like.

It should be your choice too Deepali. No need to see my comfort first.

I had never in my life visited any 5star hotel but I did with Abhay. He every time asks me before ordering something. I remember if we go to a normal hotel my dad never asks us what we want, he just used to order and we used to eat. No questions were ever asked.

After dinner, we returned home and I changed. I was about to sleep and Abhay knocked the door. I was scared why he came at this time? Does he just take me to dinner to convince me for the night? Is he also the same? Why are all boys same?

He enter to my room and before he could step further I make myself clear and said,

"See, if you think, taking me to the dinner will convince me for the night then that's simply not going to happen. Why don't you boys understand what we want? Why is sex just all you need? I just trust you and you showed your true colour. " - I yelled at him.

"Shhhh, Let me speak Deepali. I will just say one thing don't ever judge me if you have thousand of things running through your mind just ask me once and listen to my full explanation you don't ever need to judge me; from next time I assure you." And he continued.

"And about sex, We are strangers for each other and getting physical to a girl you don't know is called a slut. And I respect you and I believe that you are my wife. I treat you as my wife and I don't force you to accept me as your husband. I will wait for the time when you accept me. I don't want to treat you as a slut and have sex every night. I bought a cell phone for you so that you could talk to your friends and family. I know it's tough for you to sit at home for the entire day. I just brought a cell phone which I came to give you and nothing else. And yes, I will fix TV soon to your room so that you can watch your program if I am busy watching mine."

He gave me the phone and left the room wishing me a good night. I feel so guilty for scolding him and putting allegations on him. I was amazed at whatever he said to me. I thought about the time how my dad used to watch whatever he wants and rest of the time my mom watched what she wanted to. Does ever anyone notice what I want to do? Does ever anyone thinks about me; this much? But, yes Abhay did. This guy does the things before I demand to him. There was something in him that stopped bringing Manan's thoughts back.

I don't know despite my thoughts when I slept. The next day when I got up it's almost 9.30 am and I wondered why he didn't wake me up? He could be angry at me for behaving like this, but he always behaves calmly. I freshened up and I was sat in the drawing room. I just receive one text.

" This is me Abhay, I don't wake you up and disturb you as you were sleeping. But I must tell you that you look calm while sleeping. Rest of the time you are just ready to screw me :P. Just joking. Just save my number as you need to have your husband's number ;p . If there is any emergency call me no matter I am in the office. And I have called kantabai, she will join from today to do household stuff. and about cooking, I leave it up to you. If you feel to cook you can do or else you can confirm with kantabai she can cook for us of 2 times. And TV will be delivered by evening just sign and take delivery of it. "

I don't know why I got a smile on my face after reading his message. I am getting the care and concern which I always wanted. How he manages to take such a care for me? I decided to cook so that I don't feel alone and pass my time.

After cooking I had lots of time. It's then when I sit alone the thoughts revolves around me and make me weaker. I search for some classes on internet nearby. I find one yoga class near to the apartment. I feel strange and scared to take permission from Abhay. I don't know how he would react on this? But I somehow decided that I will convince him.

When he return home. I offer him a glass of water and he thanked me. We set for dinner and I asked him,

"Abhay, I want to seek permission from you. would you allow?" - I asked him.

"What, permission? Don't tell me you want a divorce." and he winked.

"I want to join some yoga class as I have nothing to do here except cooking. And I don't have any friends here with whom I can go out. Whenever I sit alone I get memories of Manan and believe me it's so disturbing. Till this date, I can't forgive him nor forget him. I want to join some class so that I can spend some time and get back to normal life. As you know things had affected me a lot these days."

"I guess Manan your Ex., right? what was that you can't get over it? would you like to share it with me? "- Abhay reply.

I was quiet for a moment. I don't want to tell Abhay that your wife has been used and someone has thrown her after using her. I don't want to tell him how I miss my own mom. I don't want to tell him that I want to escape from the taunt that mom gives me till this date that I have killed my own mom. I don't want to tell him about this so I keep quite.

"Okay, I don't want to force you to share something to me in which you are not even comfortable. But yes, if it bothers you so much and any day you want to spit it out

I will be always here to listen to you. I will never judge you about what you want to share. I know it was your past and I will not judge you on that I will just simply listen to you. And yes, talking about taking permission then dear you don't need to take it. It's your choice you can do anything about your life. Just inform me once what you are doing and where you are going as I am worried about you. You are now my responsibility but I don't want you to behave according to me. Do that feels you right and you want to do." - he continues further.

"I am the member of Lions club and you are my wife you just need to do registration tomorrow and you can go there. They have yoga, aerobics, swimming and many more activities. You can even have your kitty party there. You can go daily too. I will drop you there in the morning. We will do your registration and you will be a member too. And if still, you want to join that yoga class I don't mind. Be comfortable to do it."

I was quiet this time too. I was quiet as I get surprised each time. I thought I need to convince him hard but things were so opposite. This man amazed me every time. I wonder I consider this guy as my stranger but he behaves always like a guy who knows my needs and know how to make me happy.He knows what I always complain myself about not having things that other has. He knows how to make me happy and how to let me live my own life.

The next day we did registration and I joined the club. In the starting days, the lifestyle of people was so weird to me as I had never even heard about a club in my life. But soon I started liking the place. I almost every day go to the club. Abhay drop me while he leaves for the office and I return back in the cab.

One day I called Sana And asked how she is doing and about mom dad. I told her everything about here. She gets shocked that what my life is. She really is happy for me. She asked me about me any Abhay I told her that I can't accept Abhay as my husband till now but we share at least a very good bond. I told her that I started to like my life how it is now a day. I told her that I had many complaints towards my life before but Abhay is filling the space between the rocks and making the beautiful bridge to walk on.

Soon, I make many friends here. I started to hang out with them. Abhay never asked me where I was going but he always tells me to inform him. I always inform him and he never has any problem in whatever I do. I don't love him but as days pass I attracted towards his honesty, his thoughts, the way he cares for me, The way he understands me. And till theses days he never ever mentions to me that he want to get physical.

I regularly wake up and make breakfast for us and we left the house together. One day I was not well and I wake bit late and when I was about to reach kitchen I found him cooking.

"Abhay, why you are cooking? I will do that. This not comes in your job. I will make it go and get ready". - I asked him and feel guilty for giving him trouble.

"Its, not like that it's not my job you do cooking as you like it and I can do it someday if my wife is not well there is nothing that makes me down. I can do your job too if you are not well. There is not written on the wall that cooking is your job though you did it with your responsibility and here you are my responsibility too and I can do it if you don't feel better someday. By the way, how are you now?"

"How you know that I am not well? " - I asked me.

" Every day I sleep after you turn off your light just to assure that you have slept. but yesterday your light was on for such a long time and after waiting so long I came to visit and you had a fever. I called doctor he will be here soon. Just take rest today. Don't cook anything we will order something and have proper rest. "

" I was scared last night and so I turn lights on. I was not feeling well. And thank you Abhay for taking such a care for me. Now I get to know if I ever had my own mother she would take care of me just like you do. Thank you for letting me realise and giving me the feeling that I never have in my life."

" For the first time, you complimented me. Thank you. Now take rest and I will try to come as early as possible today so you don't need to stay alone. "

"Can I ask one of my friends to come here? "

"Why you ask me every time? This is your home too and you are free to call anyone I don't mind. You can party with your friends too. Invite all your friend, not one and I will order something for you guys. Enjoy and you will feel better. just update me about your health as I am concerned about it."

This time, I really was taken back by Abhay behaviour. Why this guy do this much? And in return after 4months of his marriage, I didn't even accept him as my husband.

but the fact is yes, my heart start accepting him and I start to like him. I invite my friends and that day he came early to the home and that night he was in my room for the entire night. I really started enjoying his company. I started to wait for him to return to home. I start enjoying his presence.

Days passed and things between me and Abhay were getting better. He asked me the suggestion to his business, he involves me in his important decision. I wonder if sometimes my dad had asked something to mom and if she had suggested something and it fall wrong, how dad just scolds her so hard but none of that happens between us. I really finding the real value of getting married to this person. My husband is teaching me how to live my life with pride and happiness.

There was the picnic of 2 days from the club and I have to take permission from Abhay and I don't know whether he allow me to go alone or not for 2days.

"Abhay, I want to go for tracking which is organised by club do you allow me to go? I assure you if you call me anytime and tell me to come I will come without asking anything."

"How many times I need to tell you that you don't need my permission. Can't you get that? You just need to tell me. You are not my slave that need my assurance in everything you have your choice too."

He just gets upset and walks to his room. For the first time, he got upset with me .I followed him.

I try to make him understand why every time I afraid and ask for his approval.

"Abhay, You know how I have been brought up and what they always teach me. I don't have this freedom to lead my life I wanted in my ways. Here with you, i have the completely different world. I have the world which I always wish of. But if I had ever tried to demand certain things to my parents what I get in return is anger and pain. I don't have this openness to my life to do the things of my choice. so every time I ask you. It will take some time to adapt this thing. Will you give me that time?

Before I complete he started to laugh, Baby, I was just joking. I am not angry with you. Chill. Come sit. I was just teasing you so that from next time, you don't ask or seek for any permission by hesitating.

I don't know why but for the first time I can't just resist him and I hugged him. I hugged him and cried a lot. I ask him to have a drink with me as I want to have a very long chat.

We had wine and talked for so long. I tell him everything about Manan. How he got me drunk. and used me and had sex with me and just leave me. How everyone blames me for my mom's dad. And when it's about my mom's dad I could not control and for the first time, i sob like a baby girl. I want to yell and tell everyone that I am not fucking responsible for anything.

Before I could say further he hugged me and calm me. I cried a lot. I cried that day the way I never did before. But I was sure that was the last time I am crying for my past.

You are not responsible for anything okay?. And you always want to know that why I choose you? Besides

169

knowing everything about you, why I decide to marry you? The answer is, because I find you very honest and how you tell me everything on the very first meeting attract me towards you. I get to meet the first girl who is so upfront and honest that speak openly on the face. And I can read in your eyes when I met you for the 1st time that how upset you were with your life and I want to give you your time, your happiness, if I said no to you your parent will marry you with someone who may don't understand you but I want to know you more and I was waiting until this day. I want to give you all that you never have in your life. I started liking you from the first day and now I love you even more but I don't force you.

Before he could say anything I just kissed him. He stopped me and said are you sure this is all you want and not because of this wine. I got tears in my eyes and I had no words for this man and I hugged him and kissed him so hard.
He dragged me to his bed. He removed my clothes and about to move further; I stopped him and said I am not virgin anymore. He laughed and said I though you will say , I have AIDS. And At that moment he just stole my heart. He made me fall in love with him. We made love again and again. We became one soul that never will separate again. After the 5month of marriage, I allow him to have me but this time, I am all of him just him.

My husband taught me the real value of life. He made my life what I always wanted .He teaches me to love and live with pride. He gave me freedom to fly in the sky.

170

And in all this madness of life, I don't know when this stranger became My soul.

Thank you note

First of all, I want to thank all the people who always supported me and wish for my success. I have just the idea about the concept of the anthology book but the people around me and the contributing writers actually gave the shape to the book.

My father Paresh Kaniyawala and My mother Bela Kaniyawala , always there in my ups and down and who are the ladder of success for me. My brother Ravi Kaniyawala and his wife Krishna Kaniyawala always stood by me in every step that i take. I want to thank the special person in my life who gives me the vision in writing, Who always believes in my writing and in me. They are my back bone without whom my survival is impossible.

A biggest thanks to the publisher First Step Publishing, without their guidelines the idea of book would not have turned into a memorable reality. I want to even thank all the contributing writers without whom it would have not been possible to publish this anthology book. I want to thank my colleges of my institute where I am working who always inspired me and ask me about my writing. I want to thank them who always praised me for my writing. I want to thank Radhika Mam, the best teacher I ever got who is more friend to me and who always motivates me in my studies and life .

I want to thank all my friends and readers who gave their valuable suggestions. I want to thank all the readers for picking this book and giving their valuable time to this book. This is my 1st attempt as the editor and compiler of anthology book and I hope that you all will like it. A great life to all my readers.

HAVE A GOOD READING WITH LOVE.

Ravina Kaniyawala(Riya)